THE SHUDDERING BREATH BEFORE OBLIVION

TAYLOR GRANT

CRYSTAL LAKE PUBLISHING
WHERE STORIES COME ALIVE!

Crystal Lake Publishing
www.CrystalLakePub.com

Follow us on Amazon:

WELCOME
TO ANOTHER

CRYSTAL LAKE PUBLISHING
CREATION

A GIFTED MAN

INTRODUCTION BY YVONNE NAVARRO

TAYLOR GRANT.

Wow.

I knew this guy all my life.

No, I *felt* like I knew him all my life.

I only met Taylor in person a few times, at conventions and Phoenix FanFusion. He was kind, friendly, personable, an all-around nice man. As is the downside with larger conventions, there wasn't a whole lot of time to get to know folks face to face. Still, what small amount of time we had was filled with friendly conversation. He always had a smile on his face, and that smile was always genuine.

He wrote stories, ranging from children's cartoons to horror, both psychological and visceral. He was a scriptwriter, a screenwriter, a producer, director, actor. Every story he wrote sold, no exception. And no wonder! He wrote in so many forms, from laughter to romance, from deeply disturbing psychological terror to straight out horror. You'll discover the depth of his craft in the stories collected in this book, in the connection he had with his characters in their existences and their circumstances. My personal belief has always been that a great writer actually *becomes* the character he or she creates as the story is written, and when you read the last page of the last story in this collection, and you wonder how he could have penned these words, how he could have brought these stories to life, I think you'll share that belief.

The flipside of Taylor was, in a word, incredible. He practiced all those essential and wonderful things that are often so rare and hard to find in this world today. And yet he always had them in abundance: friendship, encouragement, unabashed love. A great sense of humor and constant positivity, and *awareness*—a state of being that reminds a person that no matter what you're going through, every person around you is likely enduring some terrible thing of their own. Perception like that is as rare as an end-to-end rainbow in the midst of a sun shower. Few people have seen its magic; even fewer have stood under the rainbow's arch in the rain and felt the warmth of the sun on their face.

Taylor was like that, a welcome feeling of warmth when you needed it most. He listened, he responded. He *loved*. Even during his years-long fight against cancer, he cared for his friends, those in person and those who were virtual. Every one of them meant something. He was so thankful for them, and so amazed and grateful when they gave to him in return. He kept smiling and giving of himself no matter how much pain he went through. He shared his journey only now and then—he fought back with humor and creativity as he explored every alternative in his refusal to surrender. He endured unimaginable pain by holding on to the belief that creativity heals, being grateful for every day, and always wanting to give support and comfort to *others* despite how difficult things were for him.

If Taylor were still here, he would tell you these things:

"Empathy is a superpower."

"Kindness. It never goes out of style."

"Don't forget to be kind to yourself."

Quite a few years ago (I'm not sure when "quite a few" morphs to "many"), one of my favorite television series was called *A Gifted Man*. It was about a brilliant surgeon whose deceased ex-wife's spirit kept visiting him and convincing him to help people at the free clinic she ran. The surgeon, played by Patrick Wilson, exhibited compassion, kindness, empathy, gentleness, etc. Every time I think of *A Gifted Man*, I think of Taylor. He changed the world around him by simply being himself.

Taylor Grant was a gifted man.

Now, somewhere in the Great Beyond, he's still all those things.

TABLE OF CONTENTS

GLIMMERGRIM

CONNER SENSED HE was not alone.

Amidst the lavender-scented steam of the bathroom, he sensed something shifting, the hint of a presence felt but not seen. Though the tub's porcelain cradled him in a sea of warmth, an uneasy tension grazed his skin. A glass of Merlot was within arm's reach, a velvety promise of momentary peace.

The bath was his sanctuary from Wall Street's unyielding clock and tangled spreadsheets. An escape from the pressures of hitting targets and deadlines, even if for just a few sacred minutes.

He stared at the bath's silver fixtures—silent witnesses to his ritual of water and wine. As his gaze lingered, an unsettling metamorphosis began to take shape. The faucet, a mere shard of polished metal a moment before, began to stretch and distort into a twisted semblance of a nose. The knobs retracted into themselves, morphing into eyes that seemed to calculate his vulnerability with cold precision. A bemused chuckle slipped from his lips into the steam. "Guess I better lighten up on the wine," he murmured to himself.

But his amusement soon evaporated, to be replaced by a rising tide of apprehension. The apparition that emerged was a hideous distortion of a face, its menacing eyes sunk into the metal, its nose quivering as if it could somehow smell his fear.

He rubbed his eyes with water-softened knuckles, desperate to purge the vision. When he dared to look again, the faucet and knobs had resumed their ordinary forms, as if chiding him for his flight of fancy.

Relief washed over him.

But as his hand reached for the wine glass and another taste of sweet distraction, he froze. A face materialized beneath the water under his spread legs, its eyes two dark chasms. With a strangled cry, Conner recoiled, his sudden movement sending both water and his glass crashing to the floor.

Some of the spilled Merlot tinted the water in the bath as if blood had merged with his sanctuary, forcing him to confront the uncertain boundary between the actual and the illusory. The face wavered and slowly diffused, but its presence lingered in the room like a dark mist.

In the sterile cold of the Wall Street bullpen—a place where decimals danced, and fortunes fluttered—Conner sat at his desk, haunted. The office's chatter played like an unending Gregorian chant in the background—talk of stock rises, of market trends, of corporate mergers—but it felt like the murmuring of ghosts. A haunting liturgy to which Conner felt he no longer belonged.

For weeks now, unsettling faces were his uninvited guests, materializing at unpredictable moments, hunting him like prey. He had scoured the internet, sifting through medical journals and psychology forums, trying to find a cause or explanation.

He'd researched terms like 'hypnagogic hallucinations,' and even toyed with the idea that his symptoms aligned with some form of optical illusion or stress-induced visual phenomenon. Deep down, he wanted to believe that there was a scientific explanation for all this, that these faces were mere by-products of stress or overwork. But another part of him whispered that this was something darker, more sinister.

His makeshift defense was simple but draining: never let his gaze linger too long on any inanimate object. It seemed that the faces thrived in the stillness of his focus, particularly on reflective surfaces.

Yet maintaining constant vigilance was exhausting. His eyes felt gritty, the strain creating a constant dull ache behind his temples. He could feel his concentration fragmenting over the past few days as he attempted to juggle his work responsibilities, aware that any momentary lapse could provoke another apparition.

Around the office, co-workers were already talking about his odd behavior.

At first, the visages had limited themselves to the confines of his computer screen. But now they crept beyond digital borders.

GLIMMERGRIM

The numbers on the wall clock stretched and congealed into a sneering face.

At the water cooler, an oasis in the arid landscape of numbers and data, Conner's eyes met his reflection. Except now, even his own image stared back with a grotesque grimace. The betrayal of his own reflection hit him like a gut punch, a visceral reminder that nowhere was safe.

Back at his desk, his focus slipped for just a moment. What was normally a grid of comforting numbers and data morphed into menacing eyes that glared at him from the monitor, a malevolent entity born from the electronic void.

Nervously, he glanced around the open-plan space, wondering if anyone else could see the nightmarish vision unfolding on his screen. He glanced over at an old colleague named Bill, who was absorbed in his work, blissfully ignorant.

No, this personal haunting remained his alone.

Beth, the diligent analyst two cubicles over, whose legs could rival any Wall Street curve, caught his eye. Her look was one of unspoken concern, yet she seemed to withdraw into her work as if retreating from a contagion.

Then, in an instant, all pretense of Conner's composure shattered. A face of grotesque, near-biblical horror spawned from the pixels and darkness. As if transcending the bounds of the screen, its mouth contorted, attempting to bite him. Uttering a sharp cry, Conner's arm lashed out as he leaped up from his seat, sending the keyboard and mouse crashing to the floor.

Time froze.

Conversations halted mid-sentence. A sea of eyes turned toward him, each pair bearing its own microcosm of emotion: pity, discomfort, detached curiosity. His manager, Jerry, who was the closest, stepped up with a thinly veiled mask of managerial concern. "Conner. . .we need to talk."

Days had passed since the harrowing episode at his desk, and Conner found himself on an enforced sabbatical. "Think of it as a brief hiatus—for you and the team," Jerry, his manager, declared. He'd even had the gall to suggest a therapist, a recommendation Conner knew was less about personal well-being than it was about workplace liability.

But the isolation had its silver lining. It gave him time to delve deeper into online forums, medical journals, and psychology studies in his obsessive quest for answers. One name kept surfacing in his local area: Dr. Evelyn Stroud, a psychologist specializing in visual phenomena and repressed emotions. Intrigued, he discovered she had authored a paper titled 'The Hidden Psychology of Visual Manifestations.'

Hope swelled within him.

Devouring the content, Conner found it both unsettling and enlightening. The more he read, the more he felt as if the paper described him personally, dissecting his dread with academic precision. There was something comforting, yet unsettling, about seeing his experiences discussed in cold, analytical terms.

Emboldened by the paper's relevance, Conner reached out to Dr. Stroud via email, followed by a phone call. To his relief, she seemed just as intrigued by his experiences as he was by her research. After an in-depth phone consultation, she agreed to meet him. The feeling of being on the cusp of some kind of revelation left Conner in a state of restless anticipation.

As evening pulled its dark veil over the world, he sat shrouded in the dim light of his apartment, reading more of Dr. Stroud's paper. Suddenly, he felt a tension in the air, as if it were charged with static electricity. The lights flickered, their transient glow casting eerie shadows on the walls. Dismissing it as a power issue, he continued reading until a particularly prolonged flicker caught his attention.

For a split second, he saw a phantom face somehow emerging from the wall across from him—skeletal, ghastly, its mouth stretched in an agonizing expression. A wave of icy fear engulfed Conner, binding him to his chair. His rational mind tried to dismiss the apparition as a trick of the eye, but a low, haunting moan reverberated through the room. It was as if the wall was groaning in agony.

Rational thought clashed with raw terror.

Was the wall, or the thing, trying to communicate with him?

Or perhaps warn him?

Frozen in place, Conner contemplated fleeing the room. But as he mustered the courage, the room reverted to mundane stillness, leaving him gasping for air, his pulse racing.

He thought about his upcoming meeting with Dr. Stroud,

wishing it were sooner. He couldn't shake the feeling that each passing moment was a step closer to a new reality that couldn't be undone.

The interior of Dr. Evelyn Stroud's office felt like a separate realm, in stark contrast to Conner's sterile apartment and the Wall Street workspace. He found himself enveloped by an artful blend of rich, warm colors, classic literature on psychology, and curated artwork that beckoned one to pause and reflect.

From the moment she spoke, Dr. Stroud's demeanor was unexpectedly warm, even soothing. Her attractiveness was subtle but undeniable, quite contrary to the cold, clinical figure he had conjured in his mind. After an evaluation of his acute situation, her questions shifted from general inquiries to a more pointed, specialized probing. Her approach was as methodical as it was empathic as she guided their conversation through intricate psychological landscapes.

"I appreciate your candor and trust," Dr. Stroud said, her pen dancing across a notepad with calculated grace. "It's essential for our journey toward understanding."

She set down her pen, thoughtful. "I am reminded of symptoms of Pareidolia when the mind perceives a familiar pattern that doesn't exist. I've had patients who've seen all kinds of things—faces in the clouds, divine figures in toast. You're familiar with the 'Man in the Moon,' I presume?"

Conner nodded.

"But there's also the Troxler Effect," she continued. "Stare into a mirror long enough, and you might not recognize yourself. The brain omits the irrelevant, making the familiar strange—sometimes terrifyingly so."

Conner was struck by the clarity of Dr. Stroud's explanations, impressed by how she dissected intricate psychological concepts with ease.

"You, however, present a unique situation," she said. "Your hallucinations don't fit textbook definitions, based on what you've described, and my own research into visual and auditory manifestations."

"So, is there a pill for this?" he said, half-jokingly.

Dr. Stroud's eyes met his, filled with a compassionate yet

resolute expression. "Just to clarify, I'm a psychologist, not a psychiatrist, so I can't prescribe medication. And yes, there are antipsychotic drugs designed to help with hallucinations. But based on my diagnostic impressions, I don't believe you're schizophrenic. And medications are no guarantee. Best-case scenario, they might alleviate the symptoms temporarily, but they won't address the root issue." She paused to let the weight of her words sink in. "However, given the severity of your hallucinations, a focused and intensive treatment plan may not only be justified, but necessary."

Conner nodded. "Well, frankly, that's why I'm here, Doc. I don't have the luxury of years of traditional therapy. I feel like I'm losing my mind."

Dr. Stroud offered a comforting smile. "Let me assure you that many people find themselves overwhelmed by their thoughts and emotions at various points in their lives. I can't guarantee a 'cure,' per se, but I can promise you a committed, professional partnership to work through whatever challenges you're facing. Mental health is complex and unique to each individual, but modern treatment options have come a long way, and there's good reason to be hopeful."

After a reflective pause, her expression took on a note of reserved anticipation. "I believe we need a targeted approach to understand the intricacies of your condition. In fact, I'm spearheading an experimental project called the 'Perceptual Mapping Sphere.' It's a projective test; think of it as a much more sophisticated version of the Rorschach inkblot. It delves deeper into the subconscious mind and can give us unprecedented insights into your unique situation. If you're up for it, we can do a simple test now."

Curiosity piqued, Conner agreed.

Dr. Stroud led him to a dimly lit room with an academic feel; bookshelves lined with psychological journals and diagnostic manuals. In contrast, a spherical digital projector in the center of the room stood as a modern juxtaposition, sophisticated yet unobtrusive. The setup suggested a blend of established knowledge and cutting-edge technology.

She offered him a seat and started the projector. Clouds of swirling light materialized on the wall facing him, morphing and dissipating rapidly. "Simply relax and observe the patterns,

Conner," she instructed. "Then speak your thoughts freely." Her fingers poised over a keyboard to take notes.

Conner hesitated. "I see them. . .the faces. . .they're everywhere. They look angry, menacing."

"Remember now," she said gently, "You're only looking at a projection. They can't harm you." She adjusted a dial on the projector. The lights transformed into fractal patterns, intricate and chaotic. "What does your mind interpret now?"

"A labyrinth," Conner replied, his voice shaky. "But there are faces embedded in its walls. Male. . .female. . .adults. . .children. A mix of emotions. Too many to describe."

"Interesting. Please, go on," she said, her interest evident yet professionally controlled. She clicked a remote, and the images changed into a pulsating, singular light. "What about now?"

He spun away as if what he'd seen was too horrifying to witness. "I can't. . ."

Dr. Stroud's hand reached for the projector, switching it off, and plunging the room into total darkness except for the ambient light from her desk lamp. "What did you see?"

He wiped a tear from his eye as he said, "It was the same hideous face I saw in my office. It was lurking in that pulsating light. Waiting."

"Do you have any idea of who it was?" she asked.

"No," he said, trying to shake the image from his mind. "But whatever it was. . .it wasn't human."

⇒⟫⟫⟪⟪⇐

Leaving the office, Conner felt the twilight's chill air turn heavy. Streetlights came on, spotlighting the darkness that his mind was struggling to parse.

He saw his car parked some distance away, and the walk seemed longer now as the sky turned from twilight blue to pitch black. Then, an unnatural sound—less than a roar but more than a growl—rang out behind him. Turning, he saw it. Standing eerily still beneath a flickering streetlight was a figure, its features indiscernible yet menacingly familiar. He realized what it was: the terrifying specter from his hallucinations.

Confront the root cause, Dr. Stroud's voice echoed in his mind.

He paused and stood his ground, his breath shallow. Yet this situation felt more threatening than before, more visceral. With that same guttural sound, the figure began to crawl—slowly, ominously—toward him. Its movements were unnatural, each motion deliberate, yet still distorted.

Panic gripped Conner as he spun around and sprinted toward his car, each pounding step punctuated by his thundering heartbeat. A raspy, malevolent hiss emanated from behind him, and he dared not look back.

He yanked his keys from his pocket and nearly dropped them. A wild, guttural shriek pierced the air. He noticed a shadow gaining on him and ran even faster. Slamming into the car door, he unlocked it, jumped in, and jammed the key into the ignition. Something monstrous began to press against the driver's side window, but he didn't look. He revved the engine to life, tires screeching against the asphalt as he peeled away. In his rearview mirror, he saw the dark figure come to a halt as if letting him go.

Or perhaps postponing the inevitable.

Weeks had passed since Conner's nightmarish encounter. Given the severity of his experience, Dr. Stroud had recommended more frequent sessions, several days a week, to delve into what she believed was underlying trauma. Her office had become his haven of calm. Soft lighting, lavender scent, the predictable tick-tock of the wall clock—he needed such a sanctuary.

Today was their first foray into Regression Therapy.

"Hypnosis enables us to explore deeper layers of the subconscious," Dr. Stroud said ten minutes into their session, her eyes locking onto his. "Just remember that you'll remain in control and be safe throughout. Are you comfortable proceeding?"

"Comfortable? No. But I'm willing to try," he replied. The lingering fear in the pit of his stomach was overshadowed by a stronger urge to unearth and confront whatever lay buried in his psyche.

"Excellent," Dr. Stroud said. "Let's start by getting comfortable. Close your eyes, take a deep breath in, and as you exhale, allow yourself to begin relaxing."

Conner followed her instructions. The soft fabric of the couch seemed to embrace him as he inhaled deeply.

Her voice flowed like a soft current.

"Imagine yourself at the top of a staircase with ten steps. With each step you descend, you'll go deeper into a state of relaxation and openness. I'll count down from ten, and when I reach one, you'll be in a deep, receptive state."

Conner visualized the staircase in his mind. It was an elegant structure, bathed in a soft, diffused light. He placed his foot on the first step as Dr. Stroud began to count.

"Ten."

His foot sank into the soft carpet that covered the step, and he felt a noticeable release of tension.

"Nine."

He descended another step, the muscles in his neck and shoulders loosening, as if invisible hands were kneading away his anxiety.

"Eight."

Another step and he felt an unfamiliar lightness in his chest, a weight being gradually lifted. With each descending number, Conner moved further down the staircase and deeper into a trance. By the time Dr. Stroud reached 'one,' he was submerged in an intense state of relaxation, as though floating in a tranquil body of water, far removed from the turbulence of his daily life.

"In this deeply relaxed state," Dr. Stroud continued, her voice now hardly above a whisper, "you're able to access memories with greater ease. Let your mind drift back to your childhood, like flipping through an old photo album. Stop when you feel you've reached a moment that seems significant."

Feeling anchored by Dr. Stroud's words, Conner let himself sink deeper into the labyrinthine recesses of his mind. The room dissolved around him; the scents of lavender and leather receded, replaced by a far different smell—musty, damp like a place long forgotten.

A maelstrom of images flickered onto the theater screen of his mind, but one scene bubbled up with striking clarity. He found himself standing in front of an abandoned building, its windows shattered, the facade crumbled and peeling away. Beside him stood Liam, his childhood friend—wide-eyed and full of youthful mischief. Conner's heart raced, not from fear but from the sheer exhilaration of youthful adventure.

"What do you see?" Dr. Stroud prompted.

"It's the old Tunison building," Conner said, his voice tinged with a kind of awe. "Liam and I. . . we'd heard rumors about this place. People said the Glimmergrim haunted it. We wanted to see for ourselves. We were just kids," he said, the regret palpable in his voice.

"You're safe," Dr. Stroud said with encouragement. "Take all the time you need to experience this memory."

"We've entered the building," Conner continued, his eyes still closed, his body visibly tense on the plush couch. "It's dark, really dark, and our flashlights barely cut through the blackness. I can smell the rotting wood and crumbling bricks. We. . .start exploring, laughing nervously at every creak and groan of the old structure.

Liam moves ahead, crossing a floor that looks unstable. And then. . . Oh God, then we hear it—the howl of the Glimmergrim. My stomach twists in knots, and for a brief second, I feel light-headed, like the room is spinning around me."

Conner's hand clenched involuntarily. "Liam. . . He gets scared. He starts to back away, but then these hands. . .these horrible, inhuman hands reach up through the floorboards and yank him down into the darkness. I hear him scream and then. . .a thud. A sickening thud." Conner's voice broke, choked by an emotion he had long buried. "I. . .couldn't save him, and then I saw it, in the darkness below, staring up at me. The Glimmergrim! It was real! I ran, I had to. I left Liam, and I ran."

Then, as if the weight of the memory was too heavy to bear, Conner's eyes snapped open. He looked disoriented as if he had physically stepped back from the precipice of a dark abyss.

Dr. Stroud leaned forward, locking her gaze on Conner. His eyes were brimming with tears, a fragile veneer barely holding back years of repressed emotion. "Conner," she began, her voice imbued with empathetic warmth. "It was brave to go to that place and bring these memories into the light. They've clearly weighed heavy on your heart for a long time. This emotional journey you've embarked upon is crucial for healing."

She reached over to her side table and pulled out a box of tissues, offering it to Conner. As he wiped his eyes, she resumed the conversation. "This. . .'Glimmergrim.' Is it local folklore, or does it possess a different kind of significance for you?"

Conner swallowed hard. "When we were kids, we all thought it was a silly myth—like the bogeyman. But after that night. . .."

"It seems of great significance to you," she said. "I find it intriguing and would very much like to explore its role in your experiences further. However, let's save that for a future session. Today, the focus is on you."

She paused for a moment, contemplating her next words carefully. "Have you ever tried visualization exercises, Conner?"

He shook his head, bewildered.

"In moments when you're overwhelmed, you simply close your eyes and confront these phantoms that haunt you. Picture yourself standing strong against them, reclaiming your own narrative."

A flicker of doubt passed across his eyes, but Dr. Stroud pressed on.

"It's a mental exercise to help you gain control over what terrifies you. The power of the mind is not to be underestimated."

Conner swallowed hard. "I'm willing to try anything at this point."

"Then perhaps this exercise is the first step in confronting whatever it is you believe you encountered," she suggested, her gaze never leaving his.

A shiver coursed through Conner's body. He had come to Dr. Stroud as a last resort, putting all his hope in her expertise. But what if it failed? What if, in trying to reclaim his narrative, he only empowered the very apparitions that haunted him?

The thought left him paralyzed, weighed down by a newfound dread that maybe, just maybe, he was unlocking a door that was better left unopened.

⫸⫷

Conner sat in the back corner of the Coffee Shot, staring at his laptop screen, his eyes bloodshot, his fingers tapping nervously on the tabletop. A myriad of tabs were open on the screen, each offering pieces of lore about the urban legend known as the Glimmergrim.

Two weeks had passed since that strange regression session with Dr. Stroud, and he'd been driven by an incessant urge to unravel the threads of the monster that had resurfaced in his memory. He'd taken the doctor's advice and attempted the visualization exercises she mentioned a few times; surprisingly, it had seemed to diminish the intensity of his visions somewhat.

Yet despite the fleeting respite, he still felt tethered to the haunting entity from his past; his focus was solely on unraveling its mythology. *Glimmergrim*, the word was almost a hiss, an urban legend whispered among children but now haunting his adult life.

He had been delving into online forums, old books, and even interviews with people who claimed to have had encounters. The Glimmergrim were said to have once been human but cursed with a life of darkness and despair. Creatures that roamed urban labyrinths, drawn to the emotional intensity of teeming cities, to places where human souls 'glimmered' like a lure.

As Conner sifted through his research, he noticed patterns that extended beyond his current obsession. The Glimmergrim were part of a global tapestry of myths designed to enforce good behavior in children and serve as cautionary tales. Striking parallels existed with dark figures from other cultures, like Latin America's shape-shifting El Cucuy, the weeping La Llorona, or even the Eastern European Baba Yaga.

According to several sources, the urban legend of the Glimmergrim was wielded as a warning by parents: be home before the streetlights flicker on, and stay away from decrepit, abandoned buildings. "Don't stray after dark," they'd say. "Avoid the vacant, derelict buildings that litter the city."

These places, parents warned, were treacherous not just because of decaying structures and hidden hazards. They were also the lairs of the Glimmergrim, where they would collect the souls of the reckless and disobedient.

But Conner couldn't shake the feeling that the Glimmergrim was more than just a story. Could the faces that haunted him be the souls reaped by the Glimmergrim? And rather than haunting him, might they be warning him?

As the folklore went, if you found yourself outside after dark, the only way to save yourself was to find a reflective surface—like a puddle or a window and chant the words 'Glimmergrim, Glimmergrim, I heed your warning, please let me return home before morning.' By repeating the chant three times while looking at the reflection, it was said that you could evade the clutches of the Glimmergrim and make it safely back home.

Conner took a sip of his now cold coffee, the ritualistic words resonating in his mind.

The night Liam died; I didn't make it home safely. He thought. *Because I never did the ritual. Maybe it never stopped searching for me. And now, all these years later, it's come to collect my soul, as well.*

Just then, the cafe door jingled, and Olivia walked in, her

eyes—blue like Conner's but colder somehow—scanned the room before finally settling on him. Her features, although sharing familial resemblance with Conner, were sharper, as if years of life's vicissitudes had sculpted them to a finer point. She wore a simple but elegant blouse paired with a charcoal skirt, an ensemble that spoke of practicality but with an eye for detail. Her face, framed by faint lines, lit up with a controlled smile as their eyes met.

Conner glanced at his watch—she was punctual for once, a rare occurrence that bordered on miraculous.

"Hey, stranger," she said, her voice tinged with a warmth that barely concealed the underlying tension.

"Hey, big sis," Conner replied, rising from his chair to hug her. He felt the rigidity in her frame as they embraced, a subtle reminder of the emotional distance that had grown between them. They both sat down, and the atmosphere thickened, weighted down by a litany of words left unspoken.

After a brief interlude of awkward pleasantries and drink orders, their conversation turned to more serious matters. "I heard about your leave of absence from Mom," she said. "You OK?"

Conner fidgeted with his coffee cup, gently pushing it back and forth across the tabletop. "Not really. But I'm working on it. And to be honest, that's not what I asked you here to talk about."

"I see," she said, never one to mince words. "So, what then?"

After avoiding her eyes for an uncomfortably long moment, he found the courage to ask, "Do you remember. . .the Glimmergrim? From when we were kids?"

The randomness of the question was clear from her expression. "The Glimmer. . ." Olivia set down her drink with a puzzled look. "Is that a serious question? This is why you wanted to meet after three years of radio silence?"

Olivia's reply hung in the air like a thick cloud. They hadn't spoken since their father's death when they had argued over the funeral arrangements. It was an argument so meaningless he couldn't remember the details. But those details had never mattered; it had been a result of their own stubbornness and a lifelong power struggle coming to a head. The funeral had simply been the final nail in the coffin.

"Olivia. . .look. I'm in a bad place. You know me, I never ask for anything. But right now, I need my big sister. I need you to humor me and answer the question."

She sized him up and, after a moment, her clenched jaw loosened and her cold eyes softened. "OK, sure," she said, her eyes locking onto Conner's. "Yes, I remember. How could I forget?"

Conner sighed, and the tension in his body seemed to lessen just a notch at his sister's admission. It was as if her acknowledgment of the Glimmergrim had somehow validated the fear that haunted him. If his logical, buttoned-up sister, Olivia, remembered the bogeyman from their childhood, then perhaps he wasn't losing his mind after all.

He leaned forward and, in a bold move, reached over and held her wrist, almost pleading. "Please, Olivia. Tell me what you remember. I have these huge blank spots in my memory around that time."

She didn't remove his hand, which was a good sign. For now, it seemed, she was willing to entertain such a strange question. "Well. . .I remember you were terrified of it as a child. You and your buddy Liam would sneak out at night, and when you'd come back, you were afraid to even look in a mirror. I used to tease you endlessly about it."

Conner looked up, intrigued and surprised. "Mirrors. . .strange. I don't remember that at all."

Olivia sighed. "Well, it was a long time ago. I remember that you and Liam were always up to no good. I think they call it 'urban exploring' these days, but there wasn't really a name for it back then. You guys loved going into abandoned places you weren't supposed to. But you were both too young to understand the dangers of old buildings, so maybe it was a good thing that you were afraid of the Glimmergrim."

But after what happened to Liam. . .you became obsessed. Nightmares every night for a year, waking up in a sweat screaming about the Glimmergrim. You said you thought you were living on borrowed time because you hadn't done the ritual chant the night Liam died."

"I said that?" Conner's voice carried an undertone of disbelief, mixed with a sense of haunting revelation.

"Yes, you did. And then one day, it all just stopped. No more nightmares. And you never mentioned Liam again. It was like you locked it all away somewhere inside you."

Conner felt an involuntary shiver. His sister's words were like missing pieces in a puzzle he had long given up trying to solve.

"Olivia, I know this will probably sound insane. Hell, it probably is insane. But. . .do you think it could be real? The Glimmergrim?"

Olivia hesitated, her eyes searching his face to see if he was serious. Just then, her phone buzzed on the table. She glanced at the screen and her expression tightened. "It's work. I have to take this."

She stood and moved to another table as Conner took a sip of his cold coffee, grimaced, and put the cup back down. Olivia was whispering, but he heard her say something about "my brother" and "he's lost it."

She put her phone on mute as she returned to the table, but didn't sit down again. "I'm sorry, Con. I have to get back to the office." Then her gaze softened, clouded with concern. "I don't believe in the Glimmergrim. But I think it's real enough for you. Please consider getting some professional help, OK?"

She went back to her phone call, mouthing a silent 'I'm sorry' to Conner as she walked away.

He was left to his thoughts under the dim café light. Through the window, he watched as his sister got into her car and drove off, leaving him alone with a chill in the air and his unease. His eyes fell upon a group of kids playing in the distance. Their laughter, so carefree, so uninhibited, made him think of simpler times, times when Liam was still around.

A sense of urgency washed over him then; perhaps it was time to confront the ghosts of his past rather than skirting around them. The Glimmergrim tale, as absurd as it sounded, gave voice to his fears—fears that were no longer confined to the realms of childhood or mere superstition. What if the answers he sought lay within those very fears? Dr. Stroud's words echoed in his mind: *confront these phantoms that haunt you.*

Maybe it's time to visit some old ghosts, he thought. *Starting with you, Liam.*

Conner stood at the wrought-iron gates of St. Mary's Cemetery; his eyes drawn to the familiar rows of graves stretching toward the horizon. The twilight sun cast long shadows over the weathered tombstones, each a sentinel of eternal rest.

Taking a deep breath, he pushed open the creaking gates and made his way toward Liam's final resting place.

As he walked, he felt a weight lift off his shoulders, as if he was shedding layers of the past, but also bracing for a confrontation with whatever awaited him. Liam's grave was a modest stone marked simply with his name and the years that bookended his brief life. Conner knelt, brushing away some moist autumn leaves stuck to the gravestone.

"Hey, Liam," he whispered, "It's been too long."

As the words left his lips, he felt as though he'd unlocked a door within himself, one that had been bolted shut for years, holding back a reservoir of unshed tears and unspoken words. His voice quivered as he spoke to the cold slab of marble. "I never got to say goodbye. . .never apologized for running away that night. I wish you could see me now—how much I've changed, and how much I haven't. I'm still running, Liam, running from the goddamned Glimmergrim."

His throat tightened as if the air itself struggled to convey the gravity of his words. "I'm scared, buddy. Scared that the visions I've been having aren't just in my head. That they might be real."

Just then, a soft glow caught his eye. He looked up to see fireflies starting to emerge, dancing among the tombstones, their luminescence contrasting the ever-encroaching darkness. It was as if the universe itself was offering him a moment of respite, a poetic juxtaposition that made him think—life persists in the presence of death.

Suddenly, a gust of wind swept through the cemetery, carrying with it a distinct scent, stirring a memory. It was the earthen smell of the countless explorations he'd had with Liam in their neighborhood. He was reminded of their innocence. Children playing together, full of imagination and eager for adventure, unaware of the tragedies that would befall them. It was a potent reminder that his past wasn't just made up of fears and monsters; there was beauty there, too.

As he basked in this short-lived moment of nostalgia, a low growl reverberated through the air, shattering the tranquility. The fireflies dispersed, and the wind carried a new scent—one of rot and decay. Shadows began to elongate and distort, tendrils of darkness stretched out like dark fingers—reaching for him.

The air grew denser, almost suffocating, and he heard something circling but saw no one. A voice came from behind, as cold as a tomb's embrace, "*You. . .can't. . .run. .forever.*"

It was the Glimmergrim. Conner didn't look over his shoulder. He simply ran for his life.

It chased him. He could feel it only steps behind as he sprinted out of the cemetery gates toward his car. As he reached the vehicle and scrambled to unlock the door, he saw his own terrified reflection in the driver's side window. Behind him stood the towering figure of the Glimmergrim, its nightmarish visage only inches away. It had him where it wanted him. There was no way he could get into the car without facing it.

Something triggered within him a memory from childhood. *The ritual.* The one he never performed that fateful night. Staring at his own reflection with the monstrous thing behind him, he whispered, "Glimmergrim, Glimmergrim, I heed your warning, please let me return home before morning."

He repeated it three times and watched the demonic entity behind him fade into nothingness. He stood there for several moments. Frozen. Had that really worked?

Finally, he breathed again and spun to face whatever might be waiting for him. But he was alone. No Glimmergrim, just the parking lot of a silent cemetery bathed in the light of the rising moon and a twilight chill.

With a newfound resolve, Conner climbed into his car and revved the engine. *You can't run forever*, it had said. "You're right," he muttered to himself, acknowledging the lingering memory. *Maybe it's time to face what I've been running from.*

The respite Conner earned through the cemetery ritual was ephemeral. His life remained a theater of inescapable visions—both the ghastly Glimmergrim and the nameless faces that troubled his dreams and waking hours.

Dragged down by relentless dread, he was continually exhausted. Recognizing his fragile state, Dr. Stroud suggested a shift in their therapeutic approach. Firm in her belief that her experimental device, the Perceptual Mapping Sphere, could facilitate the unlocking of his underlying trauma, she felt this change could accelerate his journey toward recovery.

Re-entering the familiar setting of Dr. Stroud's office, Conner felt a resurgence of determination. Encircled by an intricate assembly of mirrors and cutting-edge sensors, he steeled himself to confront the specters of his past.

Maneuvering herself behind the control panel, Dr. Stroud activated the machine. The sphere hummed to life, unleashing a panoply of lights swirling across its surface, casting shadows that danced and melded on the wall. They began to morph, insinuating the outline of faces—faces that gnawed at the murky depths of Conner's subconscious.

"Describe what you see, Conner," Dr. Stroud's voice cut incisively through his reverie.

Clenching the armrests as if anchoring himself to reality, Conner replied, "Men, women, and children, their eyes wide open, their mouths wide open, as if screaming."

She jotted down some notes. "Are they the same faces?"

"Yes," he confirmed. "They're always the same faces."

"I believe they are not illusions, but rather obscured memories. Memories you've suppressed."

He swiveled toward her. "What do you mean—?"

"Don't resist this, Conner. I believe we've reached the cusp of a pivotal revelation. Please turn back toward the wall—focus on the projections."

Resigned, Conner returned his gaze to the undulating lights. He felt a nascent awareness bubbling within him, a sensation that hinted at an imminent breakthrough. Yet a shiver of apprehension coursed through him; he was uncertain whether he was ready for those revelations.

With calculated intent, Dr. Stroud manipulated the machine's settings. The lights intensified, coalescing into forms that were hauntingly familiar, almost tangible. "What do you see now, Conner?" she inquired, her voice infused with anticipation.

A searing flashback cleaved through Conner's consciousness. He was back in the derelict Tunison building, his childhood friend Liam, standing in front of him. He saw his own hands shove the boy through a gaping hole in the floor and fall to his death. A gut punch of shock and disbelief coursed through him.

"No. . .that's not what happened!" he shouted.

"What didn't happen?" Dr. Stroud inquired, tilting her head subtly as if relishing the unfolding drama.

"It wasn't me. . .the Glimmergrim killed my friend."

"Was it now," she uttered, her words forming more of a statement than a question.

GLIMMERGRIM

The haunting image persisted, looping endlessly in the crevices of his mind—an infinite loop of him pushing his best friend to a gruesome death.

Then his perspective shifted. He approached the chasm in the floor, its wood rotted and brittle. Below, enveloped in the black void, he saw eyes. Staring back was the Glimmergrim, its face twisted in a hideous smile.

"It was there," Conner whispered. "It was down in that hole. It made me do it. It *compelled* me."

As Conner's attention remained fixed on the oscillating lights, Dr. Stroud stepped closer, scrutinizing his face. "I believe you, Conner."

Tears began to stream down his face. "You—you do?"

She nodded. "I've also specialized in Anomalous Psychological Studies, differentiating the genuinely possessed from the merely delusional. And you're not delusional, Conner. You're just confused.

"I researched peer-reviewed journals on paranormal psychology. And I delved into the lore surrounding this so-called Glimmergrim. Obscure manuscripts trace its history back to a human origin, allegedly a malevolent person cursed to harvest souls to extend its unnatural life. According to myth, it can only reclaim its humanity by finding a suitable successor—a vessel already tainted by moral corruption. That, Conner, is you."

He shook his head in denial and started to rise. Shockingly, Dr. Stroud shoved him back in his seat. A sudden unease gripped him, as though the room itself had turned hostile. Her voice intensified. "You must confront your true nature. Now is the time."

The import of her words sunk in, deflating his initial defiance. His voice took on a desperate tone as he asked, "My true nature?"

With a chilling calculation replacing her usual warmth, Dr. Stroud asserted, "You wanted to do it, yes? You resented Liam; he was your better in every way—looks, courage, intellect."

His eyes vacant, Conner found himself immersed in a mental cinema, reliving those charged moments. "I. . .yes," he conceded. "I suppose. . .deep down, maybe I did resent him."

He looked up at her, distraught. "What am I?"

"*Stop* resisting," she said. "Your conscience wants to protect your fragile ego; to preserve the cognitive dissonance you achieved regarding the things you've done. Not just your childhood friend, but against all those you've murdered or harmed throughout your life. Liam was simply your first kill."

Dr. Stroud's words shattered Conner's constructed reality, laying waste to his illusions. Understanding dawned; he just needed to unlock the door to his repressed self.

And so, he did.

The floodgates opened, releasing a torrent of horrific images long contained, bursting forth into his mind like a dam giving way. The faces that had tormented him for weeks now screamed their accusations, their condemnations. Their anguished cries reverberated within his psyche.

Gripped by this shocking epiphany, he held his head as if trying to contain a mind that was fracturing.

Dr. Stroud spoke, her voice eerily composed, "Your mind fabricated false memories to create a more acceptable narrative. . .to shelter you from the truth. But you're at the mental breakpoint, Conner; what's left of your conscience has lost the war against your authentic self."

She thrust a hand mirror toward him. "Hold this. See yourself for what you truly are."

Conner was reminded of his childhood fear of mirrors. He hesitated, terrified of what awaited him.

"I said *take it*," she demanded.

His hand trembled uncontrollably as he took the mirror and faced his own reflection. What he saw there revealed the truth.

Dr. Stroud edged closer; her voice soft yet chilling. "You see now. . . don't you? Every soul carries a shadow, a secret darkness. Most deny it and lock it away, but not you. Together, we've given it life. I've been searching for someone like you my entire career. Someone who could shatter the barrier between the psychological and the paranormal."

The thing that was, once Conner, continued to gaze at its reflection. In embracing the horrifying truth, it felt a perverse sense of liberation, lips twisted into a grotesque smile.

"Come," Dr. Stroud said, extending her hand, "The world is full of. . .opportunities."

Hand in hand, they strolled through the exit, leaving behind an unsettling quiet, as if the very walls held their breath in dread of what was to come.

A SILENT KNOCK ON A FADING DOOR

MILES ARCHER FOUND the impossible hidden among the mundane: a strange glowing door in his basement. Its frame pulsated with a soft, otherworldly light, standing incongruously against the damp concrete wall. It was a stark anomaly, a fissure in the fabric of his reality.

His wife Chrissy's persistent requests, the ones that had echoed in his home's halls with a mix of frustration and resignation, had led him here.

"Clean out the basement, Miles. It's a mess," she'd demanded, her voice a constant reminder of tasks undone. He tried so hard to manage things, yet always seemed to fall short of expectations. But at this moment, as his gaze fixed on the luminescent outline of the door, Miles's world of obligations fell away, replaced by a surge of curiosity.

As a mechanical engineer, Miles had prided himself on his practicality, his ability to solve problems rooted in the tangible, the real. Yet, here was a problem that seemed to defy logic. It was as if the door, with intricate carvings and symbols that shimmered and shifted under his gaze, was a cipher, or a passage to truths still veiled in shadow.

Moving a heavy, water-damaged bookshelf had revealed the rot and decay of the wall behind it, which crumbled to expose its wondrous secret. The bookshelf, a fixture of the basement for as long as he could remember, had hidden this strange and beguiling door.

With a cautious hand, Miles reached out and touched it, the surface cool and smooth under his fingertips. It felt real, solid, yet the light that emanated from it suggested something more, something beyond. He felt a longing to understand. This might offer a way to improve his beleaguered existence. The engineer in him sought explanations in quantum mechanics, but the human in him felt the primal pull of the unknown.

At his touch, the door swung open, revealing a corridor.

"What the hell. . ." Miles murmured, half expecting a response to echo back through the shadows.

The corridor stretched into an impossible void. As he stepped through, his movement triggered a mechanism within the door frame; a digital display flickered to life, stark against the otherworldly glow: 'Remaining time: 07:59:59.'

The countdown began its descent.

Seeing those numbers, Miles felt a mix of wonder and a hint of worry. Eight hours, he thought, the concept both thrilling and daunting. The timer suggested he had a finite slice of time to dive into whatever lay beyond. Part of him was already scheming on what he could discover in those hours, while another part grew anxious at the ticking clock.

The corridor before him defied every logical explanation, a physical impossibility. Yet, it was undeniably there, as real as the cool, damp air he breathed, filled with the musty scent of forgotten things. He stepped closer, his engineer's mind racing with hypotheses, yet none could grasp the magnitude of it. The corridor, lit by a source of light he couldn't identify, seemed to pulse, its walls lined with the same intricate patterns that adorned the door. It was as if the patterns were alive, displaying a language of light and shadow that whispered secrets Miles had yet to comprehend.

Rubbing his eyes did nothing to dispel the vision. He touched the walls; they were solid under his fingers, cool and vibrating with energy. This tangible proof of the corridor's reality only deepened the mystery, adding layers of confusion and awe. Yet there was also a growing sense of dread unfurling in his stomach, a primal warning that what lay ahead was beyond the boundaries of his understanding, even beyond the boundaries of his world. It battled against a burning curiosity, a desire to know that outweighed the instinct to flee.

Behind him, the usual clutter of his basement offered a silent call to return to safety, to the life he knew. But ahead, the corridor promised answers to questions he hadn't even thought to ask. With a deep breath, Miles squared his shoulders, the decision made before he fully realized it. The allure of discovery, of understanding something so different, was irresistible.

And with that, Miles Archer crossed the threshold into a realm he couldn't have imagined only an hour before. The door behind him clicked shut, the sound final, like the snapping shut of a book.

Ahead, the corridor stretched on.

As he reached the far end, there was another identical door. As he opened it, he saw an eerily familiar sight—his own basement, virtually indistinguishable from the one he had left behind. Yet despite the sameness, a deep, unsettling feeling whispered that not everything was as it should be. The air seemed charged with an invisible tension as if reality itself held its breath.

Driven by a need to reduce the unsettling feeling and to affirm this changed world, Miles stepped through this second door and made his way out of the duplicate of his basement. Climbing the stairs, each step felt like a journey back to the familiar, yet with every moment, the sense of alteration grew stronger. Emerging into the living area, Miles paused, taking in the subtly changed surroundings.

It was his home, yet not; each detail was a mirror reflecting a life both known and unknown. Compelled by a need to confirm the reality of this world, he walked towards the front door, stepping out into the embrace of a late afternoon.

The world beyond the threshold was his neighborhood, unmistakable yet altered. The sun hung low, casting long shadows that seemed to stretch further than they should, adding a surreal quality to the moment. Across the street, old man Marco's driveway held the first tangible sign that Miles was not in his Kansas anymore. Instead of the battered pickup truck that was a fixture of the neighborhood, there sat a sleek, cherry-red sports car, gleaming under the sun's rays. It was a discordant note, a visual shout that this world operated under a different set of rules.

The sight anchored the reality of his situation—Miles was somewhere else, a place similar yet fundamentally other. The brief glimpse of the digital countdown earlier had planted a seed of urgency in his mind. He retreated back into the house, his engineer's mind cataloging the changes, trying to piece together the puzzle of this parallel world.

He spent hours exploring the house, his examination gradually becoming more methodical. He noticed small discrepancies— books he'd never read, a gadget or two less advanced than those in his world, photographs that told stories of vacations never taken and celebrations never held in his version of reality. As he took this meticulous inventory, the knowledge of the finite time-frame he had pressed at the back of his mind, sharpening his focus.

The sound of a key turning in the lock of the front door of the house froze him in his tracks.

Panic, sharp and sudden, surged through him. Heart racing, Miles scrambled for a hiding spot, squeezing into a narrow space behind a large, unfamiliar piece of furniture in the living room. Peering out, he watched as versions of Chrissy and his stepchildren, Kevin and Susan, entered, their laughter both normal and yet alien.

Miles couldn't believe his eyes. The family that entered was his, yet not. Their laughter echoed in his ears, a sound both sweet and foreign. The dissonance of watching a life so similar, yet so different from his own, was a shock to his system.

Here was a family from another dimension—his, but not.

The warmth of their interaction contrasted with the cold realization that dawned on Miles. He couldn't stay hidden forever, not with the clock ticking down on his presence here. Hunkered down, waiting for an opportunity to escape, he had to confront the reality of his situation. He was an intruder in a world that mirrored his own. Time stretched on until he heard the sound of the front door opening again.

A doppelgänger of himself stepped into the house.

The experience of seeing oneself from the outside, walking, talking, and interacting with loved ones, was overwhelming. This doppelgänger moved through the house with confidence and ease. Something Miles had always aspired to but never quite achieved. Chrissy and the kids greeted this other Miles with respect and affection, highlighting what he felt was lacking in his own life. This was more than a mirror; it was a window into what could have been.

Chrissy turned from where she was cooking in the kitchen. Her face lit up in a way that Miles hadn't experienced in years. The children punctuated their excited chatter with laughter and playful jostling as they relayed their day to this man. It was a picture of familial harmony that Miles had never managed to cultivate with his own stepchildren.

A SILENT KNOCK ON A FADING DOOR

As he watched, hidden and silent, Miles felt a burgeoning jealousy mixed with a profound sense of loss. The life he observed was his own, yet it presented a version of himself he had never become, a version that seemed to have made all the right choices, to have found a balance between ambition and happiness.

Much later, the house quieted down as everyone settled in for the night. The air in the room began to shift. It was subtle at first, a mere feeling of unease as if the world itself was holding its breath. But then, the change became tangible, a gentle pull at his clothes, his hair, like the soft insistence of an unseen current of air. The books on the shelves whispered as their pages fluttered open and closed, an ethereal breeze teasing their edges.

Alarm, a sharp and unbidden guest, rose in Miles. The house, this almost-home, was no longer silent; it was expectant, waiting for something he couldn't understand. Glancing around, he noticed the light begin to warp, the corners of the room stretching, the walls bending as if reality itself was being drawn towards a point unseen, a vortex hidden out of sight.

The realization hit him with the force of a physical blow. He was not meant to stay here. This world, as much as it shadowed his own, was rejecting his presence, an immune response to an alien element. The pull grew stronger, the sense of displacement more acute, and Miles understood that the window that had allowed his passage here was closing, fast.

Driven by instinct, he ran.

The house seemed to contort around him, hallways elongating, the usual layout turning labyrinthine in the grip of the vortex. It was a race against time, against the very fabric of this universe beginning to unravel at his continued presence.

His escape was frantic, a desperate dash through a home that felt alien. As he bolted, Chrissy, Kevin, Susan, and the other Miles caught sight of him. Their normal evening was shattered by the presence of this intruder. They immediately gave chase, confusion and fear painting their faces.

Racing through the basement door, Miles saw the corridor itself begin to narrow, the world closing in on him as if eager to eject him. Glancing back, he saw the family framed in the doorway to this other world. Their expressions were a mix of shock and horror. The corridor collapsed further, forcing Miles to duck and weave as he made his final desperate sprint.

With the last of his strength, he dove through the door to his reality, the corridor sealing shut behind him with a sound like the universe itself drawing a breath. Panting, Miles lay on the floor of his basement, the door to infinity now just a door once again.

The lesson was clear: his stay in that parallel world was finite. He had yet to understand the constraints limiting the universe's tolerance for his presence.

Miles's mind raced with questions, but also a determination. He needed to understand the rules of this game he had joined, if game it was, the science behind the door, and the implications of his actions. Was this visit a one-off? Or could he cross the threshold again? The adventure had irrevocably changed him.

Miles Archer, once a man confined by the mundanity of his existence, had glimpsed the infinite.

In the quiet of his study, Miles Archer was no longer the man he once was; he was a seeker of truths hidden within the fabric of reality. He spent his nights immersed in the glow of computer screens, delving into quantum physics theories, and exploring the endless possibilities of parallel universes. Online forums on dimensional travel and the fringes of pseudoscience became his sanctuaries, as he sought answers to the riddle posed by the quantum door in his basement.

Each journey through the door, for he discovered he could step through the door as often as he liked, offered more questions than answers, fueling a growing obsession with the mechanics of the portal and the realities it connected. Each trip was to a different version of his reality, and the same eight-hour limitation applied. Amid this quest, one question nagged at him: who had installed the quantum door in his basement? Driven by curiosity, Miles investigated his house's history. He combed through property records and looked into past owners, searching for any clues. But his search turned up empty. Nothing he found indicated anyone with the knowledge or motivation to create such an anomaly. The door's presence remained as much a mystery as the destinations it led to.

To impose order on the chaos, he began maintaining a meticulous research journal. Each entry detailed the date, time, and specific observations from his expeditions through the door.

A SILENT KNOCK ON A FADING DOOR

First, he sent inanimate objects through the portal. A clock came back with its time unchanged, suggesting no time dilation effect. A compass returned, spinning wildly, indicating abnormal magnetic fields on the other side.

Drone explorations, launched with the hope of capturing extended views of the parallel versions of his neighborhood, only offered fleeting glances before crossing the threshold. As soon as they passed through the doorway, their feeds mysteriously cut off. The brief images he did manage to capture were similar yet different from his own world. They teased with glimpses of what lay beyond but ultimately plunged his understanding further into shadow.

Beyond physical variances of the worlds beyond the door, Miles discovered startling differences in his own life's trajectory. In one reality, he was a teacher, shaping young minds with passion and dedication. Another world revealed him as an artist, his creativity finding expression in vibrant canvases. Yet another reality painted a bleak picture, showing him as a man overtaken by alcohol, his potential drowned in a sea of regret and missed opportunities.

This harrowing vision of what could have been shook Miles to his core. It served as a chilling reminder that the line between his current life and countless other possibilities was perilously thin. Each decision he made had the potential to alter the course of his life. The idea forced him to confront the very essence of who he was versus who he could become, revelations that found their way into the pages of his research journal.

To organize his findings, Miles maintained detailed records of his expeditions. Yet, with each entry, the unpredictability of each trip's effects grew more frustrating. It was about more than the alternate realities unveiled; it was also about the personal toll on him, blurring the lines between curiosity and obsession. It was a log of experiments, as well as a mirror that reflected the enormous possibilities of his existence.

It was the door's built-in timer—the strict eight-hour window for each visit—that helped narrow his focus. Moving from theoretical experiments to practical observations, the countdown emphasized the need to manage his time. Each excursion into these alternate dimensions carried the weight of these self-revelations, making the planning of his visits even more critical.

If he overstayed, the risk wasn't theoretical. Would staying past the time limit cause him to fray at the edges, as physical matter seemed to in those final moments? Would he disintegrate into the unknown? Curiosity, his constant companion, now competed with a visceral fear. It whispered to him each time he passed through the door, a perpetual reminder that beyond some thresholds, lies only the abyss.

After a half dozen trips through the gleaming doorway, Miles no longer had any doubts. What might have sounded like pure fantasy to anyone else was now his reality: each passage led to a world that held subtle differences, like variations on a theme. It felt like he was navigating through layers of existence, each a snapshot of what life could be under slightly different circumstances. The revelations were both exhilarating and humbling, offering glimpses into the boundless complexity of the cosmos and the fundamental simplicity of the human condition. With every return, the door's mystery deepened, a constant reminder of the infinite paths of life. Each branching off from decisions made and chances seized or missed.

To keep his family unaware of his newfound fixation, Miles crafted a narrative of embarking on a long-overdue basement renovation project. The excuse was thin but serviceable, granting him hours of uninterrupted time to explore the realms beyond the door. When not in use, he concealed it behind an arranged wall of old, unused furniture and boxes. An effective camouflage in the cluttered basement. This makeshift barrier was enough to deter any casual curiosity from Chrissy or the kids, keeping the door his secret alone.

Now, as he pored over his research journal, lost in the corridors of his latest theory, he heard the creak of the basement door. It heralded an all-too-familiar disruption. Chrissy's voice, tinged with the kind of trivial concern that had become the hallmark of their conversations, cascaded down the stairs. "Miles, the TV remote is missing again. Have you seen it? You know I can't watch my shows without it."

The question hung in the air, a stark reminder of the small, everyday demands that had come to define his existence. As she stepped into the messy basement, her eyes skimmed over the space where the hidden door lay concealed.

A SILENT KNOCK ON A FADING DOOR

The surge of emotion Miles felt was not only from the risk of his secret being discovered but also the mundanity of the interruption. Masking his concern with a veneer of patience, Miles responded, "I'll come look in a bit. Probably fallen between the cushions again. . ."

Chrissy peered at him for a moment longer, her gaze a mix of entitlement and the subtle accusation that always seemed to underpin her requests, before retreating upstairs. As the sound of her footsteps receded, Miles let out a breath he hadn't realized he'd been holding. The door remained his secret, but the encounter left him with a bitter taste.

In the quiet that followed, a troubling thought occurred to him. Each return from the door seemed to leave an invisible mark, a faint echo in the fabric of his reality. Was his relentless pursuit of escape weaving a subtle web of changes he was yet oblivious to?

In the silence that followed, Miles' thoughts turned inward to the life of quiet desperation he'd been leading. The marriage that had once promised companionship had soured, leaving him feeling more like a tenant than a husband. Chrissy's once-loving looks had long since turned into glares of dominance and dissatisfaction. The stepchildren, Kevin and Susan, products of Chrissy's previous marriage, offered him no affection, only reinforcing his sense of isolation within his own home.

The rundown house, once a symbol of their new life together, now felt like a prison made of debt and unfulfilled promises. Divorce, a thought that visited him more each passing day, seemed a luxury he couldn't afford, likely to leave him financially and emotionally bankrupt.

As he gazed at the glowing door, Miles realized it wasn't merely curiosity propelling him toward the worlds beyond it; it was an aching need for a place where he could reshape his existence, where respect, love, and freedom weren't just distant dreams.

And as he stood there, the glow from the door casting long shadows across the basement, a determination settled in his heart. He would cross its threshold as many times as necessary until he found a reality where he could belong.

⤜⟫⟫⟫⟪⟪⟪⤛

Dawn touched the world outside, but inside, Miles was already navigating another interdimensional journey. This time, he found himself in a basement far more opulent than his own, suggesting affluence beyond its walls.

The air was thick with an immediate sense of wrongness—a palpable tension he couldn't put his finger on. This version of the basement, though grander, carried an ominous quiet. Was he alone in this eerie stillness?

Miles moved forward. The luxury around him felt like a façade, masking darker secrets. A faint, unsettling moan broke the silence, guiding him through the shadows. Following the sound, he avoided the dark stains that marred the otherwise pristine floor—each step a confirmation of the violence that had taken place.

In the dim light of the expansive room, he discovered the source of the disturbance. It was him—or rather, another version of himself. This other Miles was bound, gagged, and bearing a gunshot wound to the chest. The blood beneath him darkened the floor. His breathing was shallow and labored, each breath a fleeting grasp at life.

Miles was stunned, the sight of himself in such dire straits freezing him in place. This was a grim lesson on the perils hidden in these alternate worlds. As he knelt beside his duplicate, his hands trembled while untying the gag, the roughness of the rope stark against his fingers.

With the gag removed and the ropes loosened, the moment's significance hit him. He stared into his own face, contorted with pain and fear, a vivid echo of the paths he might have taken. A wave of empathy overcame him; this version of him had walked roads he had not and faced choices he never encountered. The similarity of their faces made the danger deeply personal, a clear sign of the risks involved in his travels.

"G–go. . .now. . .keep that door shut. . ." the wounded Miles gasped, his voice a gravelly whisper.

Yet this desperate meeting fortified Miles' resolve. This might be a key insight into the quest he was on, emphasizing the need to understand. His sympathy for this alternate self didn't weaken him; it spurred him on to seek the truth.

"What happens after eight hours?" Miles asked, needing to know more.

Their gazes met. As the injured Miles spoke, blood trickled from his mouth. "Then. . .you can't leave. Ever," his words heavy with an acceptance of his fate.

A SILENT KNOCK ON A FADING DOOR

As the doppelgänger's breaths grew shallower, Miles searched for any last words of wisdom, any clues to the puzzle that enveloped him. "Who did this to you? Who?"

But there was nothing—only the shallow rise and fall of a chest that soon stilled forever. The other man died with many secrets, leaving Miles alone with the chilling silence of the house and the weight of unanswered questions.

Panic, now a familiar but unwelcome presence, edged into Miles' consciousness. The fear that the perpetrator might still be close sent a surge of fear through him, his skin crawling with the sensation of his own vulnerability. Compounded by the dread of the police discovering him at the scene, he realized that in this foreign world, he'd be the main suspect, perhaps imprisoned.

Reacting instinctively, with a resolve born of necessity rather than sentiment, Miles covered the body with a throw blanket. This gesture wasn't about emotion; it was an acknowledgment of their shared humanity, a connection he couldn't deny even after such a grim outcome. He then hurried back to the door, balancing urgency with caution. The relentless countdown in each dimension loomed over him—a grim reminder of the door's capricious nature, which might one day refuse his passage.

The immediate return to the familiar confines of his basement did little to quell the turmoil inside him. Standing there, Miles felt the profound impact of his actions across the multiverse. Each journey, while a desperate attempt to find a better life, might carry with it a ripple of consequences—both seen and unseen. The realization that his quest for escape had evolved into a series of morally ambiguous decisions weighed heavily on him. Despite this, however, Miles recognized a point of no return. His mission had become essential, a dogged chase for a reality where he could reshape his identity. Fueled by a mix of desperation, guilt, and a slim hope for atonement, he admitted to himself that he was fully committed to this quest. Not just to escape the life he knew, but to embrace the shadow of the man he was becoming, forever altered by the door and its secrets. With every step through its glowing frame, he felt the tether to his old self fray a bit more, the darkness of greed and ambition seeping into his psyche.

The next two days unfolded like a cascade of calamities, a relentless test of Miles's patience and fortitude. Remarkably, the source of his turmoil wasn't excursions into other realms but a weekend tasked with overseeing his dreaded stepchildren. Navigating alternate realities and facing murdered versions of himself seemed less challenging than managing Kevin and Susan while his wife was off visiting her mother. Their indifference toward him, a constant undercurrent in their interactions, had always been a source of pain. Despite Miles's attempts at warmth and connection, his efforts always seemed to dissolve into the air, solidifying the frosty divide.

Kevin, the elder, interacted with Miles only to question his authority, while Susan's disdain, echoing her brother's sentiments, felt unnervingly mature for her age. Their behavior mirrored the emotional distance cultivated by Chrissy, amplifying Miles's sense of isolation. Thrust into the deep end of parenting, he found himself navigating sibling quarrels, managing incessant demands, and maintaining a semblance of order in a household that seemed to conspire against him.

In a bid for harmony, he suggested a movie day, hoping it might offer a brief respite from shared space without conflict. They dismissed the idea with scoffs and under-the-breath critiques of his lame tastes. The day stretched on, each passing hour a marker of the growing disconnection. The role of stepfather, one he had once hoped could be filled with moments of shared laughter and learning, seemed now a part of his life marked by silent meals and colder silences.

It was against this backdrop of failure that Miles' thoughts drifted back to the door. The notion of fleeing not only his crumbling marriage but also the sting of rejection from his stepchildren had become all the more appealing. The door offered an exit, but also a path to redemption, a chance to find a world where he mattered, where the title 'stepfather' didn't signify perpetual estrangement. Silently, Miles resolved to cross the threshold again, driven not solely by the desire to escape but by the hope of discovering a place where he belonged.

As more adventures unfolded, Miles found himself pondering the widening rift between who he was and who he was becoming. With each expedition through the quantum door, not only were new worlds unveiled, but so was his discontent. He noticed a burgeoning impatience within himself, a quickness to dismiss the familiar in favor of the new and unexplored.

A month had passed, marked by ventures through the quantum door rather than days on a calendar. His excursions into unknown realms were now as routine as his morning coffee, each trip chipping away at the fabric of his everyday life. His home seemed to echo with the ghostly whispers of the lives he could be living elsewhere.

Each journey's return carried a residual trace, subtly distorting the once familiar contours of his life. First by the alienation within his home, then by the minute alterations in his surroundings—a misplaced book, an unfamiliar painting. These changes, though subtle, echoed a deeper discord, a silent herald of the unseen shifts within Miles himself.

There was also a stark change in how Miles interacted with Kevin, Susan, and particularly Chrissy. Where once there was patience, now there was a quickness to his temper, a sharpness to his replies that even he found surprising. Conflicts with Chrissy, once avoided, became more commonplace. Interestingly, their initial shock at his newfound assertiveness gave way to a kind of respect, offering Miles a sense of welcome solitude.

This assertiveness also brought with it a sense of unease. Was this shift a result of the stress from his continuous explorations, or was it indicative of a deeper, more intrinsic alteration? The thought that his journeys could be changing him was a notion Miles tried to push aside.

Lying awake in the silence of his home, Miles began to formulate a plan. His early forays, though dangerous, had always been motivated by the hope of discovery, of finding a better existence. But the reality now required a more calculated strategy. To truly find and secure his ideal world, he recognized the need for resources—resources that he didn't currently have.

Miles came to a decision in the shadowy confines of his basement, with the quantum door standing silent and expectant. Tomorrow he would continue his search for a sanctuary but also seize whatever he needed from these alternate realms. This decision, a step into moral ambiguity, was driven by desperation—a reflection of his transformation, a journey from a passive observer to an active, albeit reluctant, agent of change.

Miles stood before his workbench, the dim basement light casting long shadows across the floor. In his hands, he turned over a nondescript backpack, its fabric worn but sturdy, perfect for what he needed it to carry. Beside it lay a selection of dark clothing, chosen for stealth and mobility. He dressed methodically, each piece of clothing a layer of armor against the uncertainty of his mission.

A gun, cold and heavy, lay next to the backpack. He had picked it up during one of his adventures, a necessary precaution that now felt like an extension of his resolve.

In the quiet, his thoughts raced with anticipation and a gnawing dread. His meticulous records, once a source of scientific curiosity, now spelled out a stark reality: the window of time allowed in each alternate dimension was shrinking. What had begun as a steadfast eight-hour limit had dwindled, leaving him with only four hours for his latest excursion.

The implications were clear and dire. He was running out of time. The urgency of his situation weighed heavily upon him. The door, once his escape, had become a ticking clock, its countdown a constant whisper in his mind.

He needed resources—substantial resources—to ensure survival and comfort in whatever world he chose as his refuge. Yet, such resources were beyond the grasp of his current life. With a pragmatism borne of his dire circumstances, Miles's gaze turned to a target he never would have considered before: a quaint jewelry store in his neighborhood.

Known for its elderly, kind-hearted owners, the store had always been a fixture of community trust and the place where he had purchased Chrissy's engagement ring. It also represented an opportunity. One that Miles rationalized as being essential to his survival. The store's proximity to his home, a consistent feature across the dimensions he had visited, presented a unique advantage. He chose jewelry for its universal value across dimensions, its light weight, and ease of transport, unlike bulkier items like gold.

The simplicity of Miles's scheme belied its audacity: infiltrate swiftly, seize what jewels he could, and use the quantum door for a rapid retreat, all before anyone could intervene. The jewelry

A SILENT KNOCK ON A FADING DOOR

store's closeness to his house was strategic, ensuring the entire operation could unfold within minutes. Even if alarms sounded or security cameras captured his image, it would be of little consequence. By the time any law enforcement could respond, he'd be safely back in his basement, with the doorway to that world sealed.

Miles poured over the heist's logistics, planning each step with the meticulousness of an engineer. The elderly couple, fixtures in the local supermarkets and seen exchanging pleasantries at the car wash, had always extended to him the trust reserved for a neighbor, not just a customer. This intimacy was now a leverage point for betrayal.

The bell above the door tinkled its usual cheerful greeting as he entered, and the couple looked up from their work, their faces creasing into welcoming smiles that reminded him of every casual encounter around town. They offered to show him new pieces, but Miles politely declined, his heart hammering a frantic beat against his chest.

He watched the couple, noting their patterned dance of tasks honed by years of partnership. The man stepped into the back to answer the phone, leaving the woman to mind the store—a common occurrence that Miles had observed before and one that presented his window of opportunity.

With a deft movement, Miles opened the nearest display case, his hands steady despite the internal chaos. As he reached for a string of pearls, the woman turned, her eyes widening in shock.

"Miles? What are you. . .?" Her voice trembled, carrying the weight of shared history and the confusion of the moment.

In a breath, the situation turned. Miles straightened, his eyes locking with the woman's as his hand found the gun. "Stay back," he commanded, his voice harsh as it cut through the silent store.

She stood still, a hand raised in a feeble defense. "Please," she whispered, a word that echoed with years of neighborly familiarity.

"Turn around. Don't look at me," Miles instructed.

She complied, and at that moment, the jewelry store—their livelihood, where he had once bought a symbol of love—became just another square on the chessboard of his survival.

Time suspended as he filled his bag with the treasures that had once been tokens of celebrations and milestones. He backed away, his gaze lingering on the bowed head of the woman who had trusted him.

Miles' pulse roared, his finger trembling on the trigger. "I'm sorry," he said, the apology feeble against the gravity of his actions. "Just stay there. Don't make me do anything else."

Soon after, the quantum door whisked him back to the safety of his home world, the stones in his bag a heavy testament to the line he had just crossed. He slid to the floor, the gun clattering from his grasp, his breaths ragged with the adrenaline of escape. There, in the silence, Miles knew he couldn't undo the fear he'd instilled, the look of betrayal in the woman's eyes, and the memory of it would haunt him far more than the specter of any law.

With each successful heist, his confidence surged. The thrill of the crime, the rush of escaping through the quantum door with stolen treasures in hand, began to infect him with a dark exhilaration. It was a far cry from the life he had known, a radical departure from the man who once sought only to escape a life of quiet desperation.

Dressed in black, the nondescript backpack slung over his shoulder and the gun at his belt a chilling testament to his transformation, Miles faced the door once more, ready to step through once more. He couldn't shake the feeling that he was crossing a point of no return. But necessity drove him forward, into the glow of the quantum door, and into the unknown.

Days later, the air in the house was thick, laden with unspoken grievances and the weight of a marriage under the strain of secrets and lies. Miles felt the change within himself, too. What started as a thrilling adventure had evolved into a profound journey of self-discovery. The man staring back at him in the mirror was a stranger. The features were the same, but the eyes—they were of someone transformed by knowledge and burdened by the consequences of his actions.

Memories of love and warmth with Chrissy had faded, replaced by a void of mutual resentment and disillusionment. He missed the man he used to be, the one who believed he could be a good husband, a caring stepfather. That person was as lost to him now as the love he once shared with Chrissy.

His secretive forays through the quantum door hadn't escaped his wife's notice. The appearance of unfamiliar objects and subtle changes within their home had honed her suspicions into sharp accusatory looks, widening the gap between them.

"Chrissy, this. . .I can explain," Miles started, a vague gesture towards a set of ornate vases neither of them had purchased.

"Explain what, Miles? That our house is suddenly filling up with strangers' things? That you've changed?" Chrissy's voice cracked, her eyes darting between him and the inexplicable new additions to their decor.

A shadow of sadness softened her features, revealing the pain beneath her anger. "Do you even remember us? What we used to be? What are we now?"

The argument escalated until its breaking point, culminating in a moment of silence shattered only by Miles' fist colliding with the wall. The impact left a gaping hole, a wound in the plaster that mirrored the one in his heart.

Chrissy's fear and anger merged into a torrent of accusations. "Who are you, even? The kids, they're scared of you. I'm scared of you!"

Miles's throat tightened. The urge to confess, to reveal the existence of the quantum door and its role in their unraveling lives, tried to claw its way up his throat. But the words died on his lips, silenced by the realization that such a confession would fracture what little remained of their relationship.

Her ultimatum was brutal, her voice carrying the chill of finality, "I'm taking the kids to my mother's. It's unsafe. You're unsafe." Her eyes met his, delivering the coup de grâce. "I want a divorce, Miles. And believe me, I'll make sure I get everything."

Alone in the aftermath, the echo of the door slamming behind Chrissy and the kids reverberated through the empty house. The quantum door, once a beacon of hope, had become a symbol of his ultimate isolation.

The house felt like a mausoleum. A monument to a life once lived but now lost. Miles's resolve crystallized in the silence. He would find the life he yearned for somewhere in the multiverse. Chrissy's threats of legal action only fueled his determination. If he was to be ruined, let it be in the pursuit of something greater, not in the ashes of a life he no longer recognized.

As the night deepened, Miles stood before the door once more, this time with a sense of determination that bordered on fanaticism. In his hand, he held a gun, a blunt symbol of the lengths he was willing to go. The jewels he'd accumulated from his heists lay heavy in his bag, each gem a reminder of the sacrifices he'd made. In a quiet moment before departure, Miles acknowledged the truth: these treasures were mere stepping stones on his path to a place where he could start anew, rediscover his identity, and find peace.

The door opened at his touch, the familiar glow offering both a promise and a challenge. He glanced back at the empty house that was no longer a home, and then stepped through, the countdown ticking away the precious minutes of his dwindling window.

That same evening, Miles stepped through the quantum door for the fourth time. The now-familiar pulse of crossing dimensions wrapped around him like a cloak. He found himself in a sophisticated lab, far from the dimly lit basement he knew. The door's digital display, a constant across his journeys, sprang to life with an alarming new message: "Remaining time: 00:59:59."

The numbers began their relentless descent.

For a moment, Miles froze, transfixed by the display. The time was far shorter than usual. His windows in these alternate dimensions weren't decreasing—they were collapsing.

A man's voice caught his attention. His voice.

He spun around, instinctively reaching for the gun at his side.

The voice emanated from a corner of the room, where a large monitor cast a dim glow. On screen, a man shared his features but bore a deep scar running jagged down his face to a disfigured jawline. Despite the injury, the man managed to speak, his voice carrying a haunting, distorted quality. "The implications are far-reaching and unpredictable," the man struggled to articulate, his speech hindered by the disfigurement, yet each word was imbued with a sense of urgency and profound understanding.

Miles drew closer, intrigued and unnerved. It was clear this version of himself was not talking directly to him, that it was a recording, perhaps on an eternal loop, and one marred by glitches that hinted at its significant age. His counterpart's earnest gaze met Miles's across the divide of realities, saying, "I've seen the effects firsthand. The doors were not just bridges; they were breaches. . ."

The lab was littered with the detritus of obsession—scattered notes, humming machinery, and flickering monitors coding the air with mathematical mysteries. It was clear this place, and the man who had commandeered it had been wrestling with forces beyond conventional understanding.

Feeling the weight of his discovery, Miles became acutely aware of the timer's relentless countdown, synchronizing with his pulse. It urged him on, navigating the clutter of a journey that now seemed parallel to his own. He rifled through the notes left scattered across the lab, trying to piece together the story they told. They wove a narrative of grand aspirations, breakthroughs, and the looming shadow of unintended consequences. The quantum door, envisioned as a gateway to untold discoveries, had become a Pandora's box of quantum anomalies and existential threats.

Amid the detailed accounts of theories and trials, Miles noticed a distinct shift in the log—a personal note that took a deep dive into the existential. Written with a sense of urgency, it struck a chord: "The fabric of our reality. Disturb the balance of this too greatly, and the weave begins to unravel."

In this laboratory, the birthplace of the quantum door, Miles felt a profound sense of wonder and apprehension. He read a line that resonated deeply: "Each decision weaves a new pattern into the fabric of existence, branching into universes where alternative choices play out." The enthusiasm of these words belied the gravity of their implications. As he flipped through more pages, the tone shifted from one of discovery to foreboding. "These doors do more than connect—they tear through the fabric of reality with unfathomable consequences."

The video log continued to auto-play in the background as Miles shuffled through the papers. He was caught between the eerie admissions echoing from the screen and the insistent ticking of the countdown, a stark marker of the dwindling time. The man on the monitor, the mind behind the quantum door, shared a look of profound regret, speaking of the transformation he witnessed within himself. "The more I passed through the door. . .the less I recognized myself. We change, fundamentally, not just the world around us."

Halting the playback, Miles mulled over these revelations, seeing reflections of his own journey. The ethical compromises, the justifications for his actions—were these not signs of the same inward change?

Scattered among the personal revelations were also scientific logs, detailing experiments and theories about the quantum doors' mechanics. Its creator had come to believe that the doors did more than connect different universes, they allowed for moments of superposition. Multiple outcomes could coexist momentarily before collapsing into a single reality. This quantum entanglement, while a marvel, bore unpredictable and possibly dangerous consequences.

As Miles delved deeper, a narrative emerged from the scattered papers, revealing a turning point where curiosity veered into calamity. A single quantum fluctuation during the device's activation had opened pathways between dimensions and sparked a replication phenomenon across the multiverse. Suddenly, new doors appeared in worlds where conditions mirrored those of the original experiment—nexus points, vulnerable to the fabric of existence's distortions. This event, far from being a mere anomaly, had propagated through the multiverse.

Miles' house, and apparently countless others, sat at the heart of these junctions.

He stopped to absorb the magnitude of what he'd learned. The quantum door was not an isolated marvel but the offspring of a cosmic aberration, a direct descendant of the pioneering experiment. This 'replication event,' as termed by the creator, was an accidental byproduct of meddling with quantum states, positioning his home as a crucible in a vast network of interconnected realities.

A scribbled addition in the margin of a document caught his eye, underscoring the creator's shift from theoretical exploration to a desperate quest for redemption. "Repairing these rifts has consumed me. Perhaps I can stop the unraveling of existence itself by mending these tears." Yet, it was a final, hastily penned entry that made Miles shiver: "My only mission now is to seal the doors my hubris has flung open."

This knowledge was both a blessing and a curse, bringing Miles a sense of clarity and trepidation. It explained the surreal anomalies, the subtle yet undeniable shifts in his reality since discovering the door. His mundane existence had been thrust into the center of a cosmic drama, intertwining his fate with countless others.

This realization hit him hard. His quest for an ideal existence reflected the same hubris that gave birth to the quantum door. It seemed to reveal how each journey through the door had altered the fabric of reality as well as the fabric of his identity.

Miles saw a clear reflection of himself in the door's inventor. His initial noble quest for escape and fulfillment had paradoxically led him further away from the very connections he yearned for. Yet despite this awareness, the compulsion to continue, to press on in search of that elusive ideal world, was irresistible. He had ventured too far down this path to turn back, driven by the tantalizing possibility that his utopia might be one door away.

To stop now would render his journey meaningless, leaving him with nothing but the echo of what could have been. The sacrifices made, the lines crossed—all would be for nothing if he ceased his search when he could be on the cusp of victory.

In the silence of the lab, amidst the evidence of his and another's ambition, Miles accepted the inexorable pull of the doors. The journey ahead was not just about finding a place to call home, but about reconciling the man he had become with the man he hoped to be.

⟫⟫⟫⟪⟪⟪

Miles materialized into an unfamiliar environment that contrasted radically with the simple basement he had left behind. This was no ordinary home; the air of affluence was immediate, and tangible in the quality of the light fixtures and furnishings. His footsteps echoed on polished marble as he ventured from the basement, curiosity guiding him toward the source of faint, familial laughter that drifted down from above.

The mansion unfolded before him, each room more lavish than the last, revealing a life of unimaginable wealth and comfort. As he ascended the staircase, the laughter grew clearer, more distinct. The joyful chatter of children interspersed with a woman's melodic and warm voice.

The murmurs beckoned him. As if from a magnetic pull towards the heart of the house. Ascending the staircase, affluence was everywhere—art that spoke of centuries past, furnishings that whispered of bespoke craftsmanship. He was an intruder in this world of abundance, yet it felt like the culmination of every step he'd taken, every door he'd dared to open.

He paused at the entrance to the kitchen, the scene before him displayed like a tableau of familial harmony. A woman, who bore an uncanny resemblance to the ideal he had held in his mind, was bustling about the kitchen with effortless grace. She was talking to two children seated at a large island, plates of breakfast in front of them. The kids were laughing, engaging with their mother in a dance of morning routine that was achingly unfamiliar.

The kids noticed him first. "Hi, Dad!" they said in unison. The tone of their voices, the love imbued in them, was something he'd never experienced with his stepkids.

The woman turned, her gaze landing on him. "Hey there, back so soon from your run?" Her smile, rich with affection and a touch of amusement, filled the room. "What's with that outfit? You planning to start a new trend?" Clearly, she was his partner in this world, and the children were unmistakably his. He had never experienced a world with his biological children. They both looked just like him.

The weight of this new reality hit him with force.

He fumbled for words, a cover story forming amidst the surreal realization. "Thought I'd change things up a bit," he managed.

"Dad," the boy said with an innocent smirk. "Those clothes make you look like. . .y'know. . .a dad." The younger girl smacked her brother on the shoulder. "Don't be mean." Then she turned to Miles, protective. "I think you look good, Dad."

The simplicity of the moment, the ease of their interactions. On the surface mundane, and yet it represented everything he'd yearned for—a family that loved and accepted him, a world where he belonged.

But time was against him, the digital countdown from the door a constant shadow at his back. He had less than an hour to decide, to possibly choose this life or risk everything for the chance of something more. At first blush, this seemed like a world where they accepted him with an absence of suspicion in their eyes, offering him a sliver of hope that he could find the peace and connection he had lost—or had never truly had.

"I gotta run the kids to school, babe," the woman said, reaching her arms around his waist and rising up on her toes for a kiss. "Will you be home for dinner?"

Caught off guard by such intimacy, he stammered a yes, marveling at the exchange.

"OK," she whispered. "But are you gonna kiss me or what, weirdo?"

A SILENT KNOCK ON A FADING DOOR

The kiss they shared was brief but profound, a connection so real it frightened him. It was a promise of more, of a life filled with moments like this one.

She removed her arms then and began to usher the children to gather their things for school. Their laughter and chatter filled the space with a lightness Miles had forgotten existed.

"Give your dad hugs," the nameless woman said to the nameless children. Their farewells, peppered with their chorus of "love you" and "see you later", anchored him to the spot, long after they'd left.

Here was the dream, tangible, within his grasp.

The silence that settled in their absence was a stark reminder of the choice looming over him. He couldn't afford to waste a moment. Driven by a mix of anxiety and determination, he made his way up to the home office, a space as lavishly appointed as the rest of the house.

Miles, now seated before a computer, found himself at a familiar crossroads. This time, however, the stakes felt monumentally higher. The screen before him, a gateway to another Miles' life, awaited. He paused, a moment of introspection reminding him of the countless versions of himself he'd encountered—each with their own quirks, yet bound by a thread of shared identity. It was this thread that guided his intuition now.

He quickly guessed the password, a variation of a familiar code seen in myriad iterations of his life. This wasn't luck; it was a skill honed through countless leaps through the quantum door, a skill that connected him to the collective nuances of his other lives.

The computer granted him access to an alternate self's existence.

Miles dove into the digital records with urgency, the ticking countdown ever-present in his mind, absorbing the life of the man he contemplated replacing. He discovered this version of himself was a titan in renewable energy technologies, a pioneer whose innovations had dramatically shifted the global energy landscape. His achievements were more than commendable; they had earned him a kind of reverence and status that Miles had never come close to, despite working in the same field most of his life.

TerraEco Dynamics, the company founded by this alternate self, symbolized more than innovative energy solutions; it represented a legacy of impact and prestige. Here was a life not just of comfort but of significant contribution to society and the world—a striking contrast to the shadowy achievements Miles had accomplished in his own reality.

The gravity of his choice came into focus. Assuming this identity meant far more than merging into a new family dynamic; it entailed stepping into a sphere of remarkable influence and recognition. The moral implications cast a long shadow, yet the temptation proved overwhelming. It was more than the draw of an idyllic life that captivated him, it was also the allure of embodying a figure esteemed on a worldwide stage.

The compulsion towards this new existence was palpable. The appeal extended beyond the familial warmth and into the realms of professional triumph in an arena he was passionate about.

The decision crystallized within him. He would stay, not only for the prospect of personal fulfillment but also for the chance to assume a role of profound importance that he had always aspired to. He was ready to claim his new destiny, no matter the cost.

It was at this moment he heard the front door open and a familiar voice reached him from below.

A voice unmistakably his own.

Miles, driven by urgency, chose to face his double in the office—a space alien yet familiar, ripe for an ambush. He concealed himself behind the oak door, pulse hammering as the steps approached. The door creaked open, revealing his unsuspecting counterpart, distracted as he completed his phone call, oblivious to the imminent threat.

Miles stepped out, aiming his gun at his lookalike, who was dressed in an expensive jogging suit. "Floor, now!" His voice carried a blend of command and desperation. The alternate version of himself stared in disbelief as if his mind refused to process the sight of his own face on another man. With a stunned hesitation, he complied, lying face down on the lush carpet, his expression frozen between shock and fear.

Glancing up at Miles, the horror clear in his voice, the man stammered, "Who. . .who are you?

"I'm you," Miles replied, a stern edge to his tone. "Just follow my lead, and you'll be fine. Understand?"

A nod of bewilderment was the answer.

A SILENT KNOCK ON A FADING DOOR

Miles wasted no time securing the man's hands with a tie he had snatched from the closet. "You're going to talk. Quickly," he demanded, glancing at his watch. The seconds ticked away, each one a precious grain of sand slipping through an hourglass of opportunity.

Miles led his duplicate to the basement, a place of transition and secrets, bombarding him with questions. Personal identity, important security codes, intimate details of his life—Miles extracted as much information as he could as swiftly as he could. The doppelgänger, still reeling from the shock of being confronted by his mirror image, reluctantly divulged his life's details.

Miles's mind raced, cataloging every piece of information on his phone, every clue that could help him assume this new identity. As they moved through the lavish home, descending towards the hidden truths below, Miles took in the surrounding luxury. The art clinging to the walls, the detailed craftsmanship of the banister—each element underscored the affluence this man had garnered for himself and his family.

Soon, it would all belong to Miles.

The staircase led them downward, spiraling into the cool shadow of the basement that housed more than just the secrets of a well-lived life. Here, nestled in the underground silence, stood the enigmatic glow of the quantum door—a beacon of otherworldly light in a room where every whisper echoed against concrete and wood.

Stunned, the duplicate Miles' eyes flickered between the impossible portal and the armed man who shared his face. "What is this?" he gasped, a rational mind grasping for the logic in a scene that defied reality. "You're me. How. . .?"

"Right now, the how doesn't matter," Miles cut in, his voice as cold as the gun pressed to the duplicate's temple. "The only questions that matter are mine. So forget your confusion and start remembering. Tell me a memory, something that you've never shared with anyone else. Something only your wife would know," he demanded, his voice sharp with urgency.

The question unsettled his double, igniting an internal battle between safeguarding a private memory and self-preservation. But time was slipping away, and Miles's patience with it.

He increased the pressure of the gun barrel. "Talk, or this basement is the last thing you'll ever see." The immediate threat jolted his doppelgänger into action, and the words began to spill out, each one a piece of the puzzle Miles needed to complete the mask he would wear in this world.

"There's. . .there was this one night," he began slowly, the words seeming to cost him. "We were at the lake, just the two of us. It was supposed to be a simple getaway, but. . .I ended up confessing my fear of water. I never told anyone, not since I was a kid. But with her, it just. . .came out. She held me, right there on the dock, under the stars. She promised to help me overcome it, but. . .I never told anyone else. Not even the kids know."

As the tale unfolded, Miles absorbed every word, recognizing the potency of such a personal revelation. It was a glimpse into a moment of raw honesty and connection, a memory charged with emotional depth. This story, emblematic of genuine intimacy, was exactly what Miles needed to anchor himself convincingly in this new existence.

In the basement's dim light, shadows began their eerie dance, heralding the quantum door's impending closure. The very fabric of reality seemed to tremble, a tangible sign of the countdown's critical juncture. As Miles forged his new destiny, the air vibrated with unseen forces, the walls themselves whispering of transitions and endings.

His time to decide could be measured in seconds now, not minutes.

In that charged moment, the echo of the doppelgänger's plea hung in the air, "Why me? What did I do?" His voice, laden with confusion and fear, sought understanding in his captor's eyes.

Miles felt a moment's hesitation, the weight of what he was about to do pressing down on him with the gravity of a thousand worlds. In the silence that stretched between heartbeats, he understood that this action, once taken, could never be undone.

Yet, amidst the distortion of time and space, his resolve crystallized. "I've had more than enough of my family's drama. Your turn to play the lead."

The act of shoving his counterpart through the quantum door came with a visual cacophony—the bending of light, the stretching of shadows, and the door's glow pulsating like the heart of a dying star, signaling the end of an era and the birth of another.

The door sealed shut with a resonance that felt like the universe's final sigh, Miles was thrust back into the mansion, the quantum doorway's luminescence dimming until it vanished. The basement returned to its mundane state, yet the echo of his actions lingered.

There, in the quiet aftermath, Miles stood—a man transformed by the journey across worlds, as well as a confrontation with his deepest fears and desires, alone with a choice that would define him forever.

The following morning found Miles in the kitchen of his opulent mansion, the early light streaming through the windows, casting serene patterns across the marble countertops. He cradled his coffee, the warmth of the cup contrasting with the chill of realization that lingered beneath the surface of his newfound contentment.

He had achieved his utopia, a world where his biological children, Matthew and Jenna, greeted him with unabashed affection, and where Bella, his wife, looked at him with eyes full of love and not a trace of suspicion. Last night, their intimacy had been a culmination of his deepest desires, a moment of connection so intense it bordered on transcendent.

Now, with Bella taking the kids to school followed by a day of errands ahead, the house echoed with the silence of their departure. A sobering solitude set in. Ahead lay the daunting task of navigating a life that, while outwardly his, was marked by achievements and relationships he hadn't built. The enormity of stepping into this version of himself—esteemed in his career, a linchpin in a loving family—loomed large.

Compelled by a need to ground himself in this new reality, he drafted a message to Callie, his assistant, feigning sickness to buy time. This brief respite from the demands of his role was necessary to plan his next steps and reconcile the man he was with the man this world expected him to be.

Yes, he needed time—time to digest this whirlwind of information, to study the contours of his new existence, to undergo a crash course in assuming a new identity. Though the road ahead promised its share of discomfort and possibly moments of humiliation, the end certainly justified the means. After all, he had finally arrived at his destination.

As he ascended the grand staircase, his gaze was drawn to a

marble sculpture he had admired the previous day. A striking piece. It symbolized harmony and unity, its intertwined forms suggesting a seamless blend of strength and grace. He remembered standing before it the night before. He'd felt as if he'd finally found a visual representation of the peace and success he had long sought. The sculpture had been a beacon of his achievement, a marker that he had arrived at his utopia.

But today, something was off.

The sculpture now seemed to mock him with a subtle alteration. Its entwined forms, once fluid and harmonious, twisted into a complex knot, suggesting a silent battle. It was as if the sculpture's altered state was somehow a reflection of himself.

Shaken by this realization, Miles continued to his office, his mind racing with the implications of the sculpture's transformation. As he entered his office and prepared to immerse himself in the study of his new life, he felt a sudden, sharp blow to the head. It sent him reeling, the world around him blurring into darkness.

The last thing he saw before succumbing to unconsciousness was the silhouette of a man standing over him—a man with his face, but with eyes that held a depth of sorrow and wisdom he had yet to comprehend.

✦✦✦

Miles's head throbbed with pain. Hands and legs bound, he lay on the basement's cold floor. Before him stood a figure, a man who bore his likeness but carried the air of one who had traversed far beyond the confines of ordinary existence. His jaw was disfigured by an injury that looked old. His voice carried the weight of his trials with every word. His eyes held stories of universes untold, of cycles broken and remade.

"Hello, Miles," he began, his voice a gravelly echo of Miles's own, hindered by the impairment of his jaw. "You know who I am, don't you?"

Miles blinked several times, trying to regain his focus. "Let me take a wild guess. . . Miles Archer."

A twisted attempt at a smile crossed the other's face. "Close. I'm the one who opened Pandora's box—the creator of the quantum door."

Miles scanned the man's face, recognizing the distinct mark on his disfigured jaw. This was the man he'd seen on the video log.

A SILENT KNOCK ON A FADING DOOR

He found himself at a loss for words.

"You've traveled far, Miles," the creator rasped, each word a struggle, carrying a hint of weariness as if bearing the fatigue of countless journeys. "Your path has brought us to a critical juncture. For you. For the very fabric of existence."

Pinned to the cold floor, Miles fought through the haze of pain and bewilderment, asserting, "But why? Why now? I've finally found a place where I belong!"

The creator's sigh resonated with the burden of myriad realities. "No. Your haven is built on sand. The anomalies that keep popping up, the reality you've bent—each action pulls at the threads of existence. I envisioned the door as a tool for discovery, not as an escape from the challenges we face."

Defiance flared in Miles. "And what about you?" he challenged. "You're the architect of all of this! Your own records admit its impact on you. The door's influence. . .it's transformed me too. I didn't ask for this. None of our versions asked for this. Now look at us—both bound by your actions. But somehow I'm the one tied up like an animal!"

"Yes," the creator admitted, a rare glimpse of vulnerability crossing his marred features. "The door's opportunities change us all; in ways we can't predict. The man who built the door isn't the man standing before you. This. . .mission to correct our course, it's as much about saving others as it is about redeeming myself."

Miles's resistance wavered, the reality of their shared fate sinking in, the creator's words heavy with the cost of their shared curiosity.

"I have to rectify what's been set in motion," the disfigured man said. "For all our sakes. You're part of that clean-up."

As he stepped closer, his intentions became apparent. This wasn't an act of vengeance, but a solemn duty. The door's subtle hum, almost imperceptible, underscored the gravity of the moment.

Then the scarred man did something unexpected—he reached into his coat, pulling out a gun. The sight of it, so blunt and final, sparked a cascade of realizations in Miles. A kaleidoscope of memories erupted in his mind. The luxurious basement they were in. The high-end furniture, the marble floor, the same ropes binding him now as they had the other Miles—the one he had found shot and dying in another dimension.

It all clicked into place.

"You're going to shoot me," Miles stated, more an acknowledgment than a question. "That Miles I found before. . .that was a future me, wasn't it? I'm in a time loop."

The creator nodded, grim acceptance in his eyes, the scar etching his face seeming to deepen with the weight of his confession. "You've seen your own future, but the complexities of time travel eluded even me, at first. It wasn't until much later in my travels, after countless crossings, that I truly understood its implications. This is more than parallel worlds; it's intrinsically about time. Every journey through the door scrambles where, but also when. You've stumbled upon one of the countless paths your life could take—a path that, unfortunately, ends here, with me."

Miles tried to sit up, failed, and turned his body at an angle to face his other self. Desperation laced his voice. "But we always have a choice! It doesn't have to end this way!"

"You are not meant to be here, Miles," said the armed man. "You and I both have to face the consequences of our actions."

With that, the creator reached down and shoved a gag into Miles' mouth, tying it tightly around his head. Then, with resignation etched into the lines of his face, he raised the gun, the finality in his eyes mirroring the inescapable loop they were ensnared in.

With the gag stifling any plea, Miles lay powerless, his gaze locked on the disfigured man standing over him. The creator's hand, steady and resolute, leveled the gun. A deafening silence filled the room, punctuated only by the faint hum of the quantum door.

Then, a sharp report echoed through the basement, a sound final and irrevocable.

As darkness encroached on his vision, Miles pondered the irony—his relentless quest for a better existence had led him here, to a cold basement floor, bound and bleeding out. He was now his future self.

The cycle was complete.

A moment later, the scarred man was gone.

In the silence that followed, a question lingered, a whisper in the void: Is it truly over? Or would another Miles, drawn by the same insatiable curiosity, stumble upon him, tied and gagged, a grim warning in the relentless quest for more? Miles realized then that the door was never going to lead to salvation. It was a corridor to infinite cycles, where the end was always the beginning, and the beginning, a prelude to the end.

The quantum door hummed in the shadows. Its light flickered like a beacon through time, ever waiting.

SPECTRES

"CAN HE HEAR ME, Doctor?" the incorporeal voice asked.

A second voice answered in a direct tone. "Brain activity is now normal. Give him a few more moments to adjust—after all, there hasn't been any brain activity in ten years."

What the hell are they talking about? he thought.

Suddenly, he felt a tingling throughout his body. Smells rushed at him. Cheap aftershave. Some sort of industrial antiseptic agent. The unmistakable aroma of cigarette breath. Shapes began to form.

"Welcome back, Mr. Jackson," the first voice said.

Matt Jackson had no memories of any kind. Everything he'd learned about himself came from Bob Wheeler, his Wealth Management Consultant, and apparently, the only man on Earth who knew anything about him. Matt had no living family, no friends to speak of, and was, to his pleasant surprise, in the top 1% of the wealthiest people in America.

Matt discovered he was one of the ultra-rich; his investment portfolio included gold, high-dividend stocks, real estate and foreign currencies; he would never have to work another day in his life. His home was a secluded mansion in Malibu Canyon surrounded by 30 acres of breathtaking land.

Where had the original wealth come from? Not even Wheeler knew; he wasn't paid to know anything more than what was absolutely essential, namely manage and grow Matt's investments.

Wheeler had been the first voice he'd heard when awoken. He seemed familiar, but there were no specific memories of the man. This was to be expected, he was told by Dr. Smythe, the lead medical advisor at The Cryonic Group. Fragmented memories were a common symptom when awoken from suspended animation. It was a temporary issue, nothing to be concerned about. Smythe expected a full recovery within a matter of weeks.

The memory loss was disturbing, but he took some comfort in knowing it was temporary. Certainly, his luxurious lifestyle eased the burden. He was healthy, wealthy—and from this point forward, he could do whatever the hell he wanted.

He wandered around his immense home for several days, trying to get a sense of who he was. There were photos of him throughout the house, traveling the world with various beautiful women on his arm. He searched the Internet for more information on himself, but his personal life was an enigma; he had no blog, website, or social media presence to browse. It was downright maddening. He was also stunned at how much had changed in the world during his decade in stasis. With the wars in Afghanistan and Iraq, the ascension of China, the recession, the first African American president, high-speed Internet, Wi-Fi, smartphones. . .he could barely keep up with it all.

As he examined the trappings of his life, he felt no connection to it. It was unsettling to walk through a stranger's house when the stranger was you. The most disturbing thing was he had no idea why he had voluntarily spent ten years in a stasis chamber. Generally, they were reserved for terminal patients or those already deceased. Dr. Smythe had informed him that, despite some minimal muscular atrophy that would be addressed with a few months of physical therapy, he was in perfect health. When Matt tried to probe further as to why he had willingly gone into suspended animation, Smythe told him that it was recommended he let his memories return naturally. Forcing them back could cause unnecessary stress and emotional trauma.

He'd reluctantly accepted Smythe's advice, yet the questions nibbled at him like hungry ticks. Where did his money come from? What had happened to his family? Who the fuck was he, really? When the questions became too much to bear, his confusion grew into anger. Finally, he called Bob Wheeler in a fit of rage and threatened to fire him over the phone if he didn't tell him every goddamn thing he knew.

Wheeler finally acquiesced. He told him of a safe hidden inside a baby grand piano that sat covered in the music room of Matt's mansion. He also provided him with the digital password to open the safe. Inside, he told him, was a video recorded 10 years earlier that explained everything.

"Why all the cloak and dagger?" Matt demanded.

"I'm merely following *your* instructions prior to your ten-year sabbatical," Wheeler said. "I was told to inform you about the hidden safe six weeks after you had awoken, or if you demanded it—whichever came first."

Now, as Matt sat in front of his massive entertainment center, with a finger resting on the play button of his remote, apprehension seeped into him like water into sand. Perhaps he was better off not knowing the truth. He had tried to imagine any possible scenario that would explain why he'd gone into suspended animation—but none made sense.

He pressed the play button and leaned back stiffly on the plush leather couch.

Thirty seconds of static later, a blond, balding man appeared on the screen. His eyes were tired looking and familiar. And though his features sagged a bit, it was clear he had been an attractive man in his youth. Matt gasped when the man began to speak—for he realized he was looking at himself. The face was different, but the voice and mannerisms were his.

"Hello Matt," he heard the stranger with his voice say. Matt immediately recognized the bookcase in the background; the video had been recorded in the study upstairs.

"If you're watching this video, then most likely, you're looking for answers. What I'm about to tell you. . .well, it may not be easy for you to believe—or even understand. However, Dr. Smythe has assured me that full memory recall normally occurs within 4 to 6 weeks of being awakened.

"There's no easy way to say this, so I'm just going to tell you straight. Your given name is Frank Kingston. You're a reclusive multi-millionaire and you're dead. Well, dead to the world, that is. Ten years ago, you were in a fatal accident. Fell overboard while drunk on your yacht, *The Maximus*. Your body was never recovered."

The VCR remote dropped and clattered onto the beveled glass of the coffee table sitting in front of him. He leaned forward, his mouth slightly agape.

The video continued, "Of course none of that is true—that's just the fabricated story. Don't worry. I paid top dollar for professionals to handle everything. There's no way to trace anything back to us. I say 'us', because, of course, I am you. I'm *you* before your facial reconstruction. . .before the hair implants and the liposuction."

The man now named Matt Jackson reached up and touched his hair; gingerly running his fingers through it. Was this some kind of twisted prank?

"That's right," his former self said. "I'm what you used to look like. But thanks to the modern miracles of plastic surgery, you now look like you. All the pictures and portraits you see of yourself in the house are doctored photos. They are just part of the tapestry created to bolster our new life.

"It was necessary to start over with a completely new identity. As you can imagine, it would be much too difficult to orchestrate a multi-millionaire disappearing and then reappearing 10 years later. There would be too many questions—too many variables that could get us caught. Having us killed off and starting fresh was the cleanest, most efficient way.

"Which, of course, leads us to the most important question—why?"

Jackson was eager for information, yet fearful of what he might learn.

His former self was silent for a moment—as if preparing to deliver bad news. Finally, he said, "Why I chose suspended animation is a bit more complicated. And after you watch this tape, make sure you destroy it right aw—"

The image turned to white static.

"What the fu—" Matt yelled.

Frantic, he grabbed the remote and fast-forwarded through the entire tape.

The rest was blank.

It was like the punch line to some perverse practical joke. He noticed his wild-eyed reflection in a large mirror on the wall and began to tug at his unfamiliar features. Everything that had happened since he awoke seemed insane, and yet, as he studied his face in the mirror, he somehow knew it was all true.

Desperation gripped him. He ejected the cassette, wound the loose tape back in with one of the spools, then shoved it back into the VCR and hit the rewind button. In his ten-year absence, VCRs had become outdated technology. This was no more apparent than at this particular moment.

He watched the tape again, this time paying close attention to each and every word. But as before, the tape turned to static in the same place. Had someone erased it on purpose? And if so, why not erase the entire fucking thing?

He fast-forwarded the tape again to make sure he hadn't missed anything. This time, the tape froze. He was struck by the time code displayed on the bottom of the screen. It read 00:07:43:07.

What was it about those numbers?

Wait—*Jesus*. It was the passcode numbers to the hidden safe. Now that he thought about it, his street address had the same four numbers: 3747. If you didn't include the zeroes, all three instances had the same numbers.

Fuck this, he thought. *I'm going to get some answers.*

The Ferrari F12 Berlinetta was a beautiful machine. And according to the Ferrari website, it was the fastest and most powerful in its history, with a top speed of 210 mph. Matt pushed the Ferrari as fast as he could on the streets of Los Angeles without risking arrest, but it wasn't fast enough.

Finally, he reached Olympic Blvd and looked for the address he'd found online. The Internet had become a frighteningly useful tool in the years since he'd been asleep. A simple web search turned up Bob Wheeler's address in seconds.

It had taken a few minutes to get used to driving again; all of his muscles were still sore from disuse. But it was hardly a chore driving a $300,000 dream machine with all the bells and whistles.

He pulled up in front of Wheeler's home, parked, and glanced at the clock on his dashboard. It was nearly 10:00 PM. He didn't care. He'd taken a peek at his accounting books and seen the ungodly fees he was paying the man. As far as he was concerned, for *that* amount of money, he could show up whenever he damn well pleased. As he stomped up the front walkway, he thought about all the cryptic doubletalk he'd heard from Dr. Smythe and Bob Wheeler since he'd awoken, and he was sick to death of it. It was time to find out what the hell was going on.

Wheeler wasn't surprised to see him at his doorstep. He said he'd been expecting him. After all, Matt had no family or friends to speak of. Wheeler was his only real connection to the past.

SPECTRES

Coming to Wheeler was the obvious choice for a man desperate for answers.

The inside of the townhouse was comfortably spacious. There was nothing extravagant about the furnishings, yet Matt could see that everything was of exceptional quality. This was the home of a man who had nothing to prove. From his furnishings to the books on the shelf, everything seemed functional yet tasteful. Bob Wheeler was a man who spent his money wisely.

Now Wheeler handed him a glass of wine and sat across from him in the study.

Matt nodded his thanks and took a sip. Like everything else in the man's home, the wine was perfect.

"I'm sorry about the videotape," Wheeler said, sitting across from him and crossing his legs leisurely. "Very unfortunate, but out of my hands. You have to understand, I'm on a need-to-know basis with all of my clients. What they have or haven't done in the past is their concern. My job is to handle your present needs and to ensure your financial future.

"So you know nothing about me?"

"I'm not paid to ask questions. You gave me three specific jobs when you hired me ten years ago: manage your estate, maintain the illusion of your lifestyle for tax and accounting purposes, and arrange for you to be woken up precisely ten years after you went to sleep."

Matt polished off the rest of his wine in two large gulps and sighed heavily. He felt so helpless without his memories. His voice cracked with emotion, "It's just so. . .frustrating not knowing who you are. I feel like I'm hiding from something. It scares me."

Wheeler studied him for a long moment, and then something changed in his eyes. Matt couldn't tell if it was compassion, resignation, or perhaps a little of both. "I can imagine your frustration," Wheeler said. The good news is that, from what Dr. Smythe tells me, your memories will return within weeks.

"What I *can* tell you is that you have no criminal record and no obligations to any family or friends. Your slate is clean and your wealth is spread out globally through low-risk, high-return investments. It is an enviable position to be in, wouldn't you say?"

"Some would say that. Yes," Matt countered.

"You don't approve of your lifestyle?"

"I suppose that depends on your definition."

Wheeler laughed at that. But rather than warming his face, the laughter somehow made him look colder, crueler.

Suddenly, Matt felt the need to get out of there—and fast. Wheeler might have been efficient, professional, and a damned genius at financial planning, but one thing he wasn't—was likable.

"Thanks for your time," Matt said without offering his hand. "It's late. I'm sorry I bothered you."

Wheeler rose as leisurely as he'd sat down and gestured toward the front door. "For what you're paying me, Mr. Jackson, it's never a bother."

As Matt took his first steps down the short path toward his Ferrari, Wheeler cleared his throat and said, "There's one more thing."

Matt turned back reluctantly, not wanting to linger a moment longer. "Yes?"

Wheeler's eyes were intense. "You and I only met a few times before you went into stasis. But during our initial meeting at your house, I noticed a leather-bound journal on your desk. You were very protective of it. In fact, you hurriedly closed the book the moment I went near it. If you're looking for answers, I suspect that journal may have some for you. That is, if it still exists."

"That may be helpful. Thank you," Matt said with a terrible attempt at a grin. He turned and walked briskly toward his car.

He felt Wheeler's eyes on his back as he made his way to the driver's side door. Before climbing in, he glanced back at the man standing in the doorway, sipping from his wine glass, which under the light of the moon looked thick, dark, and viscous.

⸎

Two hours and numerous tequila shots later, Matt had managed to wash away much of the uneasiness that had driven him to the dive bar in the first place. The bartender wore an untucked chambray shirt and had the sleepy, indifferent manner you'd expect from a man who had spent too many nights witnessing the goings on of such a place.

When he first asked Matt what he wanted to drink, the answer had come naturally and without any thought. He recalled that he enjoyed tequila and Mexican beer. It was the first sign his memory was coming back, and it had provided him with a modicum of relief.

SPECTRES

Another welcome distraction was the 40-something-year-old woman sitting next to him. Far from a glamour puss, she was attractive enough; probably a knockout in her 20s, he guessed. She had a great rack, blonde hair from a bottle, and as a twice-divorcee living on alimony, admitted that she spent too much of her free time with a drink in her hand. On the plus side, she was sharp, had a sarcastic wit, and was open to seduction. When Matt mentioned that he was independently wealthy, her eyes widened slightly, and curves formed at the corners of her collagen-injected lips.

The bartender began wiping down the bar near them with a knowing look that told Matt he'd seen this scene play out on more than one occasion. "Last call, Mary Beth," he murmured, folding up his grungy bar towel.

"Thanks, Joey," she said and gave the tall man a wry grin.

First name basis, Matt thought. *That can't be good.*

Then again, he was terribly lonely and horny—mostly horny—and didn't much care about the woman's past. He wasn't in the market for a wife; he just wanted to avoid another night alone.

Mary Beth leaned in seductively and whispered in his ear. "You okay to drive?"

⟫⟫⟫⟪⟪⟪

Matt had no respect for Mary Beth, but he had to admit she was a lot of fun. She even managed to make him laugh a few times with her off-color jokes. But that laughter ended suddenly when a naked, blood-covered African American man leapt out into the street—right in front of them. Matt slammed on his brakes, causing the Ferrari to shudder violently until it stopped—missing the large man by inches.

Mary Beth slammed back into her seat. "What the hell?" she yelled.

Matt gazed into the man's terror-filled eyes. They seemed to be pleading for help.

A gunshot rang out. The left side of the man's head exploded, spraying the windshield with a fine red mist.

"Jesus Christ!" Matt punched the accelerator, hurling Mary Beth back into her seat again, tires screeching in protest.

"What is wrong with you?" she demanded.

"Me?" He shouted back, louder than he meant. He downshifted and turned onto the first residential street he saw, trying to get as much distance as possible from what he'd seen. "We could've been killed back there!"

"What? I didn't see anything!"

"You didn't—" It was clear from the look on Mary Beth's face that she was telling the truth. This was, of course, impossible, since at the very least she should have seen the blood splatter across the windshield.

What blood? Another part of his mind asked, as his eyes searched the glass for even a speck of it.

The windshield was spotless. It didn't make any sense. What the hell just happened?

"What did you see?" Mary Beth asked. "What was it?"

But Matt couldn't think of how to respond without sounding like a lunatic. If what he'd seen was real, there was no way she could've missed it. And since there was no blood residue on the windshield, he questioned whether he'd seen anything himself.

Hallucination? Dr. Smythe had warned him hallucinations were a *possible* side effect, but a remote possibility at best.

So he said, "I'm not feeling too good. I should take you home."

And he did.

⟫⟫⟪⟪

Mary Beth lived adjacent to Beverly Hills in a small, but well-kept, two-story condo. Matt's intention had been to drop her off and go home, but she'd insisted he come in for a drink. He wasn't sure if she was an unusually forgiving person or just desperate to get laid—but he decided not to examine it too closely.

A night with an attractive stranger sure as hell beat going home to an empty bed. And if he were lucky, it just might take his mind off that man's exploding head. He and Mary Beth enjoyed a couple more drinks together, which helped take the edge off.

Matt was lost in thought when a seductive whisper from behind him said, "Care to join me?"

He turned just in time to catch a glimpse of blonde hair and Mary Beth's black negligee as she wafted into the master bedroom.

He downed the rest of his drink like a shot and set the glass down—right next to a stack of bills on a vintage patina table. His eyes widened as he caught a glimpse of the numbers in Mary Beth's address: 3747.

Those same four numbers again. A different order—but they were the same four numbers all right.

Matt wasn't superstitious—at least he didn't think he was—but something wasn't right. Every shred of intuition told him to get out of there. He took a deep breath, ran his fingers through his hair, and prepared to ask for a rain check.

The master bedroom was dark and quiet; the moon cast eerie shadows through the window over a large four-poster bed that took up most of the space.

"Listen. . ." he said, and his voice cracked when he said it. "I'm not feeling well and—"

The blood everywhere stopped him cold; it looked as if someone had sprayed the walls with it using a hose.

But that wasn't the worst part.

Mary Beth's body was splayed across the bed; it had been split open from her neck down. Her glistening intestines were stretched out from her abdomen and had been used to tie her arms and legs to the bedposts.

And then somehow, impossibly. . . the dead woman turned her broken neck into an impossible angle until her bloated face was grinning at him with a knowing look.

It wasn't Mary Beth.

Matt fell back and screamed; he smashed into a bookcase and caused it to collapse with a crash.

The door to the master bedroom's bathroom flung open and Mary Beth came scrambling out, wild-eyed. She was still wearing the black negligee and holding a silver-handled brush matted with blonde hair.

Matt glanced over at the bed and saw it was empty and perfectly made.

"Are you fucking crazy?" Mary Beth yelled.

He didn't answer her; he was too busy running from her home.

Matt spent the next two days at home in a drunken haze, taking advantage of the full bar at his disposal. But no amount of alcohol could wash away the hallucinations, which had become increasingly gruesome; every conceivable kind of torture and mutilation, visited upon an array of ghostly victims, without any context. He had placed several frantic calls to Dr. Smythe, but according to his unhelpful answering service, the good doctor was out of the country for several weeks on business.

In between drunken rages and bouts of uncontrollable sobbing, Matt searched every nook and cranny of his sizable mansion for the journal Wheeler had described. Not finding it only spurred more outrage and drunkenness.

On the third day, he woke up on top of the billiards table in the game room with a loaded gun in his hand. He'd found it the night before, hidden behind some bottles on the top shelf of his bar. He carried it around the house for several hours and had seriously considered using it on himself—then passed out.

Now, as he glanced around the game room, there was a growing sense of familiarity. And despite a horrendous hangover, that familiarity made him feel a little better. He glanced at a *Star Wars* pinball machine in the corner, and suddenly remembered the day he'd got the high score. A rack of CDs against the wall, including the entire *Led Zeppelin* collection, brought back pleasant memories, too. He could feel his identity returning, moment by precious moment. Carnal images flashed through his mind. There had been women, oh yes. He could see their faces in a twisted kaleidoscope of memories, each perversion more disturbing than the last.

What kind of person had he been? Curiosity ate at him, yet he was afraid to look too closely. Another flash of memory and he remembered hiding other weapons besides the gun. Yes. . .he *was* starting to remember! He could see an image. . .a dungeon of some kind.

He leapt to his feet and began to run—it was all coming back now. There was a hidden room built beneath the house, only accessible by a trap door. As soon as he reached the study in the northernmost room of the first floor, he knew exactly where to look. He knelt down, grabbed the edge of a massive Oriental rug, and flipped it over.

He recognized a particular floorboard and yanked it loose. Underneath was a small but sturdy wooden handle. His fingers wrapped around it like an eager python and he heaved the trapdoor open, revealing a set of dust-covered steps leading down into a pool of darkness.

Nothing good would come from going down there. Somehow, he knew this. And yet, he also knew it was inevitable that he would descend.

As he stepped down into the blackness, he remembered a light switch at the bottom of the stairs. He braced himself as he turned on the lights. It didn't make a bit of difference; what he saw there shook him to his core. In that one moment of recognition, he knew that despite his new name, new face, and fabricated life, nothing could change what he was and always would be.

Matt found the journal Wheeler had described in a locked cabinet against the back wall of the secret room. It didn't take long to figure out the lock combination: 3-7-47.

Inside the cabinet were stacks upon stacks of journals—some going back hundreds of years. Some were written on tattered notepads, while others sported fine leather covers. The oldest was written on parchment.

He spent all day and that night poring through them and the intimate details of nine different people's lives, starting in the mid-1600s and ending ten years prior, the day he went into suspended animation.

He was all of them. Only the names and circumstances had changed.

James Dowle, his original name, a Puritan from East Anglia in England, had moved his family—his wife and two children—to Salem, Massachusetts in 1676. His unfortunate streak of luck began with the loss of his wife Abigail to smallpox in early '77, followed by his 6-year-old son Isaac and 4-year-old daughter Mary. He soon contracted the sickness too, and in desperation, sought out a healer reputed to cure the incurable—for a price.

A secret meeting was planned, as this was not long before the Salem witch trials, and any unorthodox practices at that time were suspect. He paid the old woman his entire life's savings for a powerful spell of healing.

To his amazement, it worked.

Having survived the smallpox scare, Dowle came up with a plan to reclaim the money he'd paid the old hag. He showed up at her home one evening a week later, demanding that she return his money—otherwise, he threatened to accuse her of practicing witchcraft, a crime punishable by death. When she refused, he slit her throat and ransacked her home, stealing a small fortune, and an ancient book containing everything from love spells to good fortune hexes, to demonic curses.

It was at this point, while reading the first and oldest journal, that Matt finally remembered the significance of the numbers that had been haunting him. April 3rd, 1677 (4/3/77) was the date Dowle had used the book of spells to summon a powerful and nameless demon. It appeared to him as a formless entity, like living black smoke. The only discernible features were its nine glowing eyes, which glowed like burning embers. It promised him nine lives of wealth, power, and influence, as well as the retention of his memories from each previous life. Upon his ninth death, the demon would return to claim his soul.

To maintain the spell's effects, Dowle was required to sacrifice a human being once a year on the anniversary of the pact. This pleased him greatly, as it gave him the excuse he needed to unleash the bloodlust he'd suppressed his entire life. He far exceeded the amount of killing necessary to maintain his pact; his list of victims throughout his nine lives numbered in the thousands.

With great wealth came the ability to build secret torture chambers, constructed within the depths of his castles, châteaux, and colonial mansions over the next few centuries. His positions of power and influence generally kept him above suspicion. And on the rare occasion that he had come under scrutiny, he'd used his vast resources to pay off, discredit, or kill anyone whom he considered a threat.

Throughout all nine lives, he had searched for a loophole in the demon's pact, and finally, in his life as multi-millionaire Frank Kingston, he had. A combination of technology and mystical knowledge was his salvation; a way to project his soul—by releasing it into the limbo between life and death. The answer was suspended animation; a way to cause all bodily functions to cease and untether his soul from its human vessel. It would be out of reach of the demon, forcing it to return to its dimension empty-handed, unless it was ever summoned again.

The plan had worked. Goddamn if it hadn't! Now he was unfrozen and alive again, free of the demon and eager to enter a new pact—with a different entity. He glanced around at the dungeon he'd built and examined some of the torturous devices lined up against the bloodstained walls: thumbscrews, a Pear of Anguish, a Breast Ripper—even a custom-made Iron Maiden. Memories of the men, women, and children he'd tortured mercilessly and slain floated through his mind. Recollections came slowly at first—like spectres. He remembered the nigger who had managed to escape the dungeon in his colonial mansion that night in 1803. He'd quickly caught up to the man and blown his brains out on the private road leading to his plantation. This was the spectral reenactment he'd witnessed on the highway a few days ago. Not a hallucination. Not a ghost.

He recalled the woman he'd seen sliced open in Mary Beth's bedroom. In a previous life as a brothel owner in Paris, he had choked the woman to death with her own intestines. She had dared to scratch his face when he'd tried to rape her and he'd made her pay for it dearly. He had loved that woman; or something as close to love as he could fathom.

He pushed those thoughts out of his mind. He was now more vulnerable than he'd been in centuries. Without the protection of a pact, if he somehow died, he wouldn't be resurrected a tenth time. He needed to summon another demon quickly, and that would require a fresh kill. Perhaps that whore Mary Beth he'd met in the bar. She lived alone; she was an easy target. Then again, that bartender who had seen them together might remember his face if the police investigated—so perhaps that wasn't the best idea.

A phone rang from upstairs, startling him. It was the first time he'd heard it. Who could be calling at this time of night?

He raced up the stairs to catch the caller before they hung up, excited at the prospect of someone from his past calling.

"Hello?" he said breathlessly into the receiver.

Silence.

Straining, he could hear breathing on the other end of the line.

"Who is this?" Matt demanded.

"Dr. Smythe," a familiar voice answered.

Matt ground his teeth. "About goddamn time you returned my call."

"Listen," the doctor said. "I need to see you right away. I have to talk to you in person. The phone isn't safe."

Matt said, "Isn't safe? What are you—"

"Tonight at the clinic. I'm the only one on duty."

Matt grew more suspicious. "I want answers, Smythe."

"Don't worry. You'll get them. . .I know things."

The next thing Matt heard was a dial tone.

Matt struggled to remember any details about Dr. Smythe— certain parts of his memory still remained fuzzy. He vaguely remembered procuring the doctor's services and paying him a king's ransom for his discretion.

He wondered how he'd found Smythe in the first place—possibly through Wheeler.

I know things. Those were his last words on the phone. Matt didn't like the implication; if Smythe knew anything incriminating, he would have to be disposed of.

Matt grabbed his gun before he left, realizing this new situation might work to his advantage. After all, he needed a fresh victim to summon a demon again.

Matt arrived at the clinic an hour later to find the front door unlocked and wide open.

He'd already been tense, but now he was getting downright jumpy. He didn't like being exposed in this way; he liked more control over his victims. He reached into the large front pocket of his winter coat and wrapped his hands around the Glock .9mm hidden there.

"Hello," he called out as he entered the tenebrous, empty lobby. His voice echoed back, cold and hollow. Matt felt the walls by the door for a light switch but found none.

In his left hand, he carried a knapsack filled with the specific materials he would need to conjure another demon. The dungeon in his mansion had been filled with every conceivable herb, root, gemstone, aromatic, and occult ingredient imaginable. The sooner he could enter into a new pact, the better. He wasn't comfortable in his current unprotected state; for the first time in centuries, death would be permanent.

He locked the clinic door from the inside and pulled out his gun. There was an oddly familiar scent in the air, but he couldn't quite place it. "Dr. Smythe!" he called out and ventured deeper into the shadows.

Despite the uncomfortably cold temperature, sweat slid down his temples. He started to think he'd made a mistake coming here in the first place but realized he'd probably never get a better chance at the doctor alone.

He moved farther into the darkened hallway; it was dimly lit at the other end by what he guessed was a red light just beyond his view. It cast a faint, eerie glow across the walls. His throat felt more constricted with each step he took.

SPECTRES

A moment later, he nearly cried out in fear when he noticed a dark figure standing motionless at the end of the hall.

It was a nude female with long, disheveled hair backlit in crimson.

"Hel. . .hello," he croaked, his throat feeling bone dry.

The figure remained deathly still.

"Look, I don't know who you are, but I've got a gun." *Where the hell was Smythe?*

A hideous, unidentifiable sound erupted from the woman's throat, and she began to move toward him. When the light caught her just right, he could see that her face had been savagely carved off.

He had done that to many pretty girls.

Yet this hallucination didn't vanish quickly, like the previous ones had. As she drew closer with outstretched arms, he could smell her rotting corpse. He fired his gun and a bullet blew a hole through her neck, exposing the cartilage and muscle underneath. The faceless woman staggered from the impact, and then reached for him again—her fingers curled like claws.

Matt took a step back, about to fire at her again, when he felt a terrible pain in his right calf. A boy drenched in blood—no more than 5 years old—was biting into his leg like a wild animal.

He shot several bullets into the child's head until it resembled the remains of a smashed bowl that had been filled with jelly. He took note that the lower half of the young boy was missing. The little bastard was one of countless children he'd torn in two on the rack over the centuries. It was one of his great delights. But the sight of it now—rotted flesh, and all—was turning his stomach.

At the end of the hall, more silhouettes appeared. Four. . .then eight. . .then so many he lost count. A handful of them were headless.

He emptied his rounds into the growing horde and watched some of them jerk back as the bullets slammed into them. The sound of gunfire in the confined space stung his ears.

Silently, they kept coming.

He felt his knapsack slip from his fingers. . .heard the contents spill onto the ground. But he ignored it, his thoughts only on survival now.

He ran the other way, wincing at the bleeding wound in his calf. How could a hallucination bite him like that? *It wasn't possible!*

As he raced for the lobby, he noticed more lumbering figures blocking his path—trying to cut him off.

He veered toward the right and into another dark hallway, panic rising in him. *Godammit, there has to be an emergency exit!*

Just ahead was a glass door; *Authorized Personnel Only* was emblazoned on it.

He hit the door running and it swung open wide. He recognized where he was immediately: the main chamber for body storage. He spun and closed the door, locking it from the inside. The chilly temperature in the room was almost painful; he huddled into his jacket for warmth. The rows of cryo-units reminded him of shiny, metal coffins. A wave of claustrophobia swept over him; he had spent a decade inside one of those loathsome things.

The mob of animated corpses reached the thick glass door and began to claw at it, smearing it with blood and other bodily fluids. The face of a young girl in front was smashed against the glass; there were two jagged holes where her eyes used to be.

The door wouldn't hold them for long.

A strange, unearthly sound emanated from behind him. He spun around to see thick black smoke swirling around him as if alive. He recognized it immediately and started to scream—but it caught in his throat, his vocal cords paralyzed. In fact, he couldn't move any muscles at all.

Smoke continued to gather like the clouds of a terrible storm and formed into a human shape—that of Dr. Smythe. His hardened face twitched and his lips gave way to the faintest hint of satisfaction.

"Don't you think it's time to end this charade?" Smythe said, and the voice was as cold as his narrowed eyes. He appeared to float toward Matt, stopping barely an inch from his face. The stench caused him to choke; a smell he now recognized as sulfur. It was exuding from the demon's mouth.

"Your double cross was well-thought-out," it said. "I'll give you that. But you didn't read our contract, did you? It binds us in every way—we are symbiotic. I was aware of your deceitful plans the moment you thought of them.

"In fact, I'm not here. I'm in your mind. Everything you've experienced is by design, an intricate drama starring you as the lead, while everyone you've encountered were extras and supporting players. I gave you the worst thing imaginable. . .the hope of happiness and freedom. . .just so I could strip it all away and reveal the truth of what you really are.”

Tears began to spill from Matt's eyes. For he knew that everything the nameless demon said was true.

“I can read your thoughts now. You're terrified of going back into that cryo-unit for all of eternity.” A grin spread across the demon's face. “But that's the best part.”

Matt struggled to understand.

“Don't you see?” the demon laughed. “You never left it to begin with.”

It was then that Matt noticed the silver nameplate above the nearest cryo-unit. It read:

CRYO-UNIT 7734
MATTHEW JACKSON
STATUS: IN STASIS

Matt was no longer a tangible form. He felt his consciousness still *inside* the cryo-unit. He struggled against it, desperate to maintain the illusion, to keep his physical form outside the metal coffin.

The cold fear of what was coming rose in him; trapped forever inside his body, unable to move, yet conscious of every moment.

There had been no hallucinations. *He* was the hallucination.

As the last of his consciousness returned to the darkness of the stasis chamber, his vision inverted. From this new perspective, he saw the engraved numbers on his nameplate and finally understood their true meaning.

His mind began to scream.

7734 upside down spelled *hell*.

RED CHRISTMAS

I T WAS SAFER in the darkness.

For Gabby, it was a refuge from the screaming, the anger, and the violence.

She was still small and nimble enough to burrow into the farthest corner of the closet. A sanctuary amidst shadows and storage boxes.

Squeaky, a golden-brown hamster, was curled in her lap next to Ruby Rose, a unicorn plushie. She gave both a light squeeze to let them know how much she loved them.

The screaming and violence continued.

Gabby could make out certain words, though she didn't understand all of them. "Bankruptcy" and "foreclosure" were foreign concepts, but the word "cheating" came up a lot as well. Gabby often wondered what game her mom had cheated on that would make her dad so angry.

Something crashed against a wall, the sudden shock striking somewhere inside Gabby's chest. Squeaky uttered a single *squeak*.

"Shhh," Gabby whispered in the blackness, stroking the hamster's back.

Soon there was a familiar hacking noise from her mother, as if a dog were choking up a bone. Then came the whimpering cry.

Gabby let out a deep breath. She could tell this particular battle was nearly over.

She gently placed Squeaky onto a folded quilt her grandma had sewn and reached underneath to grab the flashlight she kept hidden there.

The hamster's ears were up, whiskers twitching, large round eyes blending into the darkness. Gabby snapped the light on, lifted

RED CHRISTMAS

the nearest box's lid, and pulled out various items her grandma had left behind.

There was a set of teacups, a pair of horn-rimmed glasses, a harmonica, newspaper clippings, a photo album, and other odds and ends. There were also some well-worn books with their pleasing musty smell.

Most of the books were too advanced for Gabby's reading skills, but they made her feel closer to her grandma at a time when her heart ached with grief. Her beloved protector had passed away two months ago after a long illness, and Gabby felt as if she had lost her life raft in a raging storm.

As she reached the bottom of the box, she took note of the only book she hadn't browsed before. It had no title and was heavy with a red cloth cover. Inside, she spotted an envelope inscribed with a single handwritten word: Gabby.

Her expression changed from morose to sheer delight as she opened it. Inside was a handwritten letter from her grandma, purposely written in simple language the young girl would understand. Grandma had known Gabby struggled a bit with reading and spelling, suffering as she did from a mild form of dyslexia, and she still needed to "sound out" words, which often took some time.

The letter read:

Hi angel,

Your mom and dad don't believe in magic, but of course, you and I do. So, I've written out a prayer for you to prove magic is real.

I know I promised you a Christmas present, but sadly, it looks like I may not be with you this year. Instead, please accept this magic prayer as my gift.

If you believe in miracles, they can come true! Make sure to read the attached prayer out loud on Christmas Eve—you'll see how magical life can be.

Remember, you must BELIEVE.

I love you with all my heart.

Grandma
PS. Keep this letter and book a secret!

Tears brightened Gabby's eyes and made them glitter like dark stars in the night sky. She wiped at them, skimming through the prayer, which was all about Santa Claus, magic, and the power of belief.

Christmas had been one of the few joys of Gabby's short life. Flying reindeer. Elves. A generous, plump man who came bearing gifts one miraculous night per year. She embraced it all.

Though her parents were not ones for flights of fancy, her grandma had spent years weaving wonderful tales of Jolly ol' St. Nick. And true to Grandma's word, Santa had always left something Gabby wanted under the Christmas tree each year.

Her parents seemed to despise Christmas as much as they despised each other. But due to persistent urgings from her grandma, they had resigned themselves to going along with the holiday year after year.

This year, on the other hand, was looking bleak. Without Grandma's influence, her parents hadn't put up a single decoration.

Gabby missed the bright, beautiful Christmas tree most of all.

Her mom had said coldly, "We can't afford one this year. Get over it." When Gabby had cried, her mom backhanded her, sending her crashing into the kitchen table and cutting her upper lip.

But Gabby didn't want to dwell on that. She began deciphering her grandma's prayer. After all, tomorrow night was Christmas Eve, and this was her chance to bring peace to her home with the power of magic.

⋙✦⋘

The following day, Gabby spent most of it in her room reciting the prayer repeatedly.

As night fell, she peeked out of her bedroom window and was astonished to see snow spilling down like quiet feathers. *The prayer worked!* She thought. For she'd never experienced a white Christmas in real life and stood in wonder as snow danced in the night air.

Neither of Gabby's parents had said a word to her since breakfast, which was just as well. The silence was a welcome alternative to the screaming. She remembered the famous line from the book *Night Before Christmas*, which her grandma had read to her many times. *'Twas the night before Christmas, when all through the house, not a creature was stirring, not even a mouse.*

That line had partly inspired Gabby's Christmas wish. No toys. No pretty dresses. Just a quiet, peaceful home.

That was when she saw the shadow pass across her bedroom window.

"Santa?" she uttered quietly, pressing her nose against the frigid glass.

She immediately spotted a tall, gaunt figure on the front lawn, cast in shadow. There was a flash of what looked like a red suit, and the silhouette of a beard, but that was where similarities to Santa ended.

The skeletal figure looked inhumanly tall, with odd-shaped limbs that stretched unnaturally. He dropped to the snow-covered ground and *slithered* toward her two-story house.

Gabby's initial delight had turned to fear. The reddish Santa-thing began to crawl up the side of the house like a spider. . .straight towards her bedroom window.

Backing away in horror, she watched as it began to ooze through the tiny space between the bottom sash and the sill. She'd always wondered how Santa entered homes without chimneys, and the answer was now clear. He poured through the slit-like bright red blood and reconstituted inside her room.

Inexplicably, the scream that had been building in her throat dissipated the moment he offered his disarming grin. In his eyes, there seemed to be an understanding. As if he knew her pain intimately and was there to take it away.

She didn't flinch when he reached out with elongated fingers and placed them gently on her shoulder. Instinctively, she knew he wasn't going to hurt her.

This wasn't Santa, of course.

It was Satan.

With her mild dyslexia, Gabby occasionally reversed letters. And unbeknownst to her, the prayers' multiple references to "Old Nick" were definitely not the same as St. Nick.

Old Nick glanced down then, seemingly impressed by the ancient evocation symbol on the floor drawn with fresh, innocent blood. Gabby had prepared it exactly as the details of the prayer had instructed.

She had noticed many such symbols in her grandma's untitled book with the red cloth cover. The text, however, remained indecipherable, since it was written in a different language.

In the center of the symbol were the bloodied remains of her beloved Squeaky, who had sacrificed his life just a short time ago. Gabby had hidden the small carpenter's ax she'd used in the back of the closet.

"You've done well, Gabby," said Old Nick.

She gathered her courage and said, "My parents are downstairs drinking wine and watching TV."

"Indeed," he grinned knowingly.

Gabby watched, awestruck, as his exceptionally long fingers sprouted black claws, like those of a fierce bird, right before her eyes.

A grin spread across the young girl's face. "Can I watch?"

Old Nick gave a rich, full-throated laugh, and his eyes sparkled with delight. "You are a special one, aren't you?" He gestured for the door. "Lead the way, young lady."

Gabby felt special at that moment, and more importantly, she felt safe in his presence. Much like her closet sanctuary, she felt safer in the darkness. Perhaps she might help her new guardian more in the future and benefit from his continued protection.

Moments later, they headed downstairs to see Gabby's parents about her Christmas wish.

There would, of course, be terrible, anguished screams and blood-splattered walls. But by Christmas morning, Gabby would receive her wish of long-lasting peace at home.

PREY

THE NIGHT WAS full of shapes. Dark on dark. But shifting. Crawling.

He ran.

The moon hung like a neon scythe, casting the barest of light over the ruins of the city, the towering spires that once reached for the heavens now crumbled with decay.

Dr. Marcus Johnson heard a familiar skittering nearby; the terror of it propelled him toward a partially collapsed building. His heart pounded as he squeezed through a narrow gap in a deteriorated wall, scraping his arm badly.

He didn't dare to cry out.

Inside, the air was heavy with dust and the faint smell of rot. Moonlight filtered through broken windows, casting eerie shadows across the desolate interior. He moved deeper into the dilapidated structure, the building's former purpose indiscernible.

Blood seeped down his forearm onto his hand.

Hide! He thought. *Before they smell it.*

Ahead, through the gloom, he could make out what appeared to be a storage room, its once gleaming door now hanging loosely.

A moment later, he heard a cacophony of skittering and chittering on the roof.

Marcus rushed through the darkened doorway. The storage room was cramped, filled with discarded equipment and the remnants of a once highly advanced civilization.

In the corner, he found a gap between a collapsed row of machinery. It was a tight squeeze, but it would conceal him well enough. He hoped.

He heard them moving along the roof and the walls, chirping in their hideous alien language.

Stupid. How could I have been so goddamned stupid?

He'd lost track of time in his desperate search for hyperconductive wiring and failed to make it back to base camp before nocturnal predators crawled out from the cracks and crevices of the world.

Then again, without the wiring, he was as good as dead anyway. The Chronosphere that time-shifted him thousands of years into the future had been damaged during his latest exploratory mission, the result of lightning from an unexpected storm. Marcus needed hyperconductive wiring to repair it. Otherwise, he'd be trapped forever in this post-apocalyptic nightmare.

Since his arrival a week ago, he'd scoured the remnants of several abandoned technological facilities and one research laboratory. To his dismay, the technology he uncovered was far too advanced to be compatible with his time machine.

His only hope was to locate a historical museum or tech archive that might have something he could salvage.

The one hint of good luck he'd had was his success harvesting rainwater. He'd created several catchment areas with containers he found and created a simple filtration and purification system using a layer of fine mesh.

The rain had been plentiful, but unreliable. If things dried up, he would be in serious trouble. Yet the precious water he'd stored was back at his makeshift base camp several miles away. He wouldn't be able to reach it until daylight when the city's chittering predators scuttled back to their darkened haunts.

Just then, his stomach growled so loudly he feared they might hear it. He hadn't eaten since his arrival and was burdened with a relentless headache, a weakened body, and a mind becoming less sharp by the day.

It would be impossible to repair the Chronosphere if he couldn't think straight. There had to be some sort of canned or packaged consumables within the abandoned city. Surely the former denizens of this once-sophisticated metropolis had figured out ways to preserve food.

There were abundant indigenous plants, but he had no way to discern between toxic and edible. If he became desperate enough, he might have to try some and hope for the best.

Or he could eat bugs.

PREY

He shivered at the thought.

He promised himself to make sustenance his top priority the following day.

If he survived the night.

He woke to the sound of chittering.

The monstrous thing stared at him in the faint light, its reddish-brown exoskeleton gleamed. Marcus threw his hand over his mouth to contain the scream.

It was one of them. A cockroach the size of a bobcat.

The sight of its enormity froze Marcus in place, primal fear taking hold.

Quivering antennae, delicate yet powerful, waved with an eerie rhythm in the air, twitching and probing the environment, sensing the tiniest disturbances.

But it was the mandibles that seized Marcus' attention, their jagged edges moving with a disturbingly fluid grace, accompanied by menacing snaps and clacks.

Marcus was all too familiar with roaches. They had been instrumental in the early tests of time travel. Their durability and adaptability made them perfect test subjects, and they were six to fifteen times more resistant to radiation than humans.

He hypothesized that the mutated cockroaches he'd seen infesting the city were descendants from his lab's countless time travel experiments. The implications were too horrible to imagine.

And while he respected roaches' adaptability, he loathed them with equal measure. They were big, greasy, and thrived in the dark. Not to mention their cannibalistic tendencies, how they thrived in filth and spread disease. They were supernaturally fast and nearly indestructible, having survived for millions of years. Plus, they could regrow lost limbs and live without their heads for weeks.

Live without their heads. For weeks. They were like tiny monsters dreamt up by a demented God.

But the one facing him now wasn't so tiny. The repulsive thing jerked toward him; its eyes, a pair of dark, glistening orbs, radiated eerie intelligence that defied the natural order. Marcus reached for the salvaged metal shard he kept shoved under his belt. It was a primitive weapon, but it was all he had.

He knew the roach's exoskeleton would be resistant to piercing strikes, so he focused his gaze on its vulnerable underbelly. The insect's wings, normally hidden and folded against its segmented body, unfurled with an unsettling swiftness. Marcus watched in horror as it spread them, each delicate membrane expanding to reveal a vast expanse.

The insect launched itself at him, wings beating a frantic rhythm.

With a surge of adrenaline, Marcus delivered a swift but well-aimed blow. The shard of metal became an extension of his wild determination to live. As he struck at it, over and over again, the cockroach recoiled and convulsed. Its intricate network of muscles contorted uncontrollably, causing its spiny legs to fold in against its armored frame.

A final tremor coursed through the dying creature's body; its appendages locked in a final, macabre pose. Silence settled upon the room, broken only by Marcus' labored breaths.

He stared at the insect's chitinous shell: once a fortress against the world, now a dead husk.

He would remove it with his metal shard.

And God help him, he would eat.

The horizon blazed with hues of pale gold and soft lavender, casting a gentle glow on the desolate streets. Marcus had searched three buildings and come up empty-handed. Eating the giant roach had managed to be even more horrible than he'd imagined. But he'd survived the experience and felt stronger having had a meal.

As he turned a corner to the next thoroughfare, he gasped.

Six people were moving toward him. They were dressed in what appeared to be containment suits, resembling bulky armor.

Marcus sprinted toward them, waving his hands, overjoyed to see other survivors.

"Hey!" he shouted. "Hey there!"

All six halted abruptly.

The tallest member of the group stood his ground while the others took a step back.

"Oh, thank God," Marcus breathed, tears of relief welling in his eyes.

The tallest of the group raised his hand, as if in greeting.

But Marcus' joy turned to horror when he saw the man draw a weapon. A flash, and everything went black.

PREY

Marcus awoke to the sound of buzzing. It took him several moments to orient himself to the sterile room. He'd been stripped naked and bound to what he deduced was an operating table.

The buzzing emanated from an automated medical device that had lowered from the ceiling just above him. Its metal appendages resembled long arms with hands, gripping what appeared to be surgical instruments.

Images of the countless live roaches he'd dissected in his lab flashed through his mind. Had they felt like this?

He noticed movement in his peripheral vision and looked to his right. Beyond the large observation window was theater seating. A crowd dressed in armored containment suits gathered to witness the procedure.

Marcus heard a voice over a loudspeaker, but it was muffled through the window and he couldn't make out the words.

The audience began removing their metallic hoods.

They appeared to be mutated humans of some kind. Their skin was waxy and unnaturally smooth, lacking subtle variations of individuality and humanity. Pallid to the point of translucency, they were uniformly fragile looking, perhaps why they needed the armored suits.

Their eyes were all too human, though, and they watched Marcus with utter revulsion. Their hybrid antennae probed the air, and their glistening mandibles twitched and flexed.

Marcus was already screaming when the operation began.

SEVEN WAYS
TO BURY A MAN

MY HAND SEIZED the steering wheel, a sharp pain stabbing through my shoulder—a memento of bones knit with steel and sheer will. I flexed my fingers, feeling the ghost of my injuries. Yet, I welcomed the discomfort; its jagged edge kept me sharp.

I'd shadowed Alex Jennings all day. At least that was the name he was going by now. Under the brim of a baseball cap, my ponytail was tucked away, a simple disguise aiding my anonymity. The neighborhood slept, the air thick with a storm's promise, but the real test wasn't the steady constant throb in my back, abetted by the pain in my shoulder—it was waiting for justice.

I sipped my coffee and winced. Nothing like a cold cup of bitterness to complement the evening's entertainment. Two weeks of this, staking out his place in my rental car, tracking his every calculated move. I varied my spots, sometimes situating myself blocks away, merging into the city's hum of delivery trucks and the constant buzz of pedestrians. I stayed under the radar, swapping cars, and changing my looks. So far, these tactics allowed me to watch his personal and professional life closely.

He was adept at the dance of wealth and power. His latest mark, Carrie Bristol, was a recent heiress who seemed blind to the danger she was in. Carrie had inherited her parents' extensive assets and business interests after their sudden and mysterious deaths, deaths that may or may not have been set up by Alex. But I only had suspicions on that front, no tangible proof.

Yet.

Alex had quickly positioned himself as Carrie's trusted

investment advisor and an indispensable ally—much like he had with me years ago. It was that damned gravitas and charisma he'd honed over the years. He knew how to use them as weapons of distraction, while his target remained tragically unaware of his true nature. He was an expert at weaving his influence into both personal and financial decisions.

Take it from me, I'd know.

The pain in my bones surged, threatening to overwhelm me. I reached for the pill bottle in the glove compartment, the rattle a familiar sound in the quiet of the car. With a practiced ease, I popped two of the painkillers and chugged them down with the last of my cold coffee. Medication was a necessary evil. It kept me functional, short-circuiting the pain at its worst.

The night stretched on, and I found myself longing for the worn, daffodil-print lounge chair back home in Summit County, Colorado. My place wasn't grand, but it was mine, and it was damn comfortable—in sharp contrast to the cramped seats of the rental cars I'd endured for nearly four weeks in Los Angeles. They only intensified my usual pains. Yet, watching Alex's house reminded me of why I'd traveled so far. It fueled a need far stronger than any physical pain could counter.

As I watched the quiet house, shadows from my past crept into my thoughts, pulling me back to a pivotal night over a month ago. I was holed up in a short-term rental where Mulholland Drive murmurs secrets to Laurel Canyon, back when I was still getting decent sleep in the shadow of Hollywood's elite. I was in town following a lead in my ongoing hunt for a man named Drew Coleman.

The man who had changed everything.

That night, I was mindlessly flipping through TV channels when I caught a local business news segment. There he was—Alex Jennings, touted as an investment prodigy. Something about his smile caught my attention, maybe the familiar wrinkles at his eyes. It jogged my memory. It was him—Drew, alive and flourishing under a new alias.

The TV framed his altered features, his attempt at disguise meager at best. His sandy blonde hair was now a deep chestnut, but his distinctive sharp jawline and piercing blue eyes were something I'd never forget. He'd tried a beard too, a feeble effort really, to soften his face's harsher lines. But he couldn't hide the chilling intensity of his gaze.

Despite his attempts at disguise, Drew Coleman was unmistakable beneath those superficial changes. The television blared about his financial exploits, showcasing how he managed the fortunes of L.A.'s elite, including Carrie Bristol, a newly minted heiress. It all clicked then; the pattern was too familiar, the method unmistakable. I recorded the segment with my phone, my heart hammering with each second. That video became a crucial piece in my expanding dossier, igniting a fresh wave of determination.

The next day, I extended my stay in the City of Angels indefinitely, shifting my focus. I was set on unraveling the truth about Drew Coleman, now masquerading as Alex Jennings.

At first glance, his relationship with Carrie seemed almost too polished, like a sitcom couple whose smiles were a bit too bright, hiding their drama until the cameras stopped rolling—except, in this script, I knew where the bodies were buried.

And then, as if on cue, everything changed when Anya, his hidden paramour, appeared. In retrospect, I suppose it was inevitable that his authentic self would surface. The gentlemanly facade he presented to Carrie was just that—a mask. I knew it all too well. His darker side he reserved for Anya and their covert trysts.

I felt for Carrie; she was as blind as I had once been.

From the safety of my car, I had watched as Anya stepped into the center of Alex's shadowy theater—a naïve Russian model dreaming of the catwalk. Like many before her, she was ensnared by Alex's brooding allure and suave deceptions.

In the last couple of weeks, I had observed them in the hidden corners of restaurant VIP sections and behind the shaded windows of lavish cars. His demeanor was deceptively caring, yet unmistakably predatory. The girl looked barely out of high school, and as I watched her step onto the porch of Alex's abode just now, she seemed hesitant, her laughter piercing the night shrilly. Alex followed her, ever the seducer, steadied her with just a touch. Their kiss lingered, a private moment brazenly displayed for a night-cloaked audience.

Each photo I snapped added to the mosaic of Alex's treachery. I reclined in my seat, the camera's cold metal contrasting with the burning in my chest. He had spun a web that ensnared both Carrie and Anya, much as he had once trapped me.

A sudden rap on my window snapped me back. I looked up to

see a security guard peering in, his brow beaded with sweat despite the cool night air. He was young, his uniform slightly disheveled, marked by a vivid splash of ketchup on his sleeve—his sheepish glance told me he knew I'd noticed.

"Evening, ma'am. Everything all right here?" His attempt at wiping the stain was futile; it just smeared further, adding to his embarrassment.

"Just lost in thought," I replied, masking my annoyance with a calm I didn't feel.

He tried to maintain a professional demeanor. "We've had some concerns about your car sitting here for a while," he stated, his voice steady though his hands fidgeted, dabbing at the ketchup again.

His flashlight swept over the mess on my passenger seat, pausing on the camera. It was a silent reprimand; a reminder of my not-so-invisible presence. I could see he had more to ask, but I wasn't in the mood. "I appreciate your concern. I was just leaving," I assured him, managing a smile that didn't reach my eyes, and pulled away.

He stepped back, inspecting the bright smear on his shirt. After another futile attempt at cleaning it, he shrugged and rolled up his sleeve, concealing the stain. Ah, if only hiding in plain sight was as easy as hiding a ketchup stain.

As his figure dwindled in my rearview mirror, the fading lights cast long shadows, reminding me of the flaws in my current approach. It was a cue to shift gears—from the tangible streets to the intangible world online. Tomorrow, I would begin sowing digital seeds of suspicion and plant them amidst his inner circle, cultivating them from behind my laptop screen.

As I blended back into the city's rhythm, my purpose sharpened; the digital landscape awaited, a domain where secrets are unlocked not with keys but with clicks.

As I drove towards a budget hotel I'd scoped out earlier, the low fuel indicator flickered to life, yanking me from my reverie. This mundane task was yet another reminder of my physical limitations. I veered into the nearest gas station, its harsh fluorescent lights slicing through the darkness.

Stepping from the car, my limp whispered of past fractures, a soft but insistent echo of my brokenness. As I unscrewed the gas cap and gripped the pump, an intense pain shot through my shoulder. It was in these ordinary moments, performing daily chores, that my injuries made their presence most known. Each squeeze of the trigger of the pump sent a ripple of discomfort from my shoulder down to my wrist, echoing the pain of countless hours of physical therapy I'd endured.

"Focus on what you can control," my physical therapist used to say in those first months after I'd emerged from my coma when I was still trying to coax movement from my shattered hands.

I caught my reflection in the car window just then. The woman staring back, sculpted by sheer determination, bore little resemblance to the patient I was just two years ago. Hell, I barely recognized myself.

The drive that followed was a silent communion, the city lights smearing into streaks as I steered towards what would serve as my hotel and new base of operations. Alone with my thoughts, I pondered the transformation within me. Once, I was Audrey Moore, deeply embedded in a life filled with love, innovation, and family dreams. I led a thriving tech startup, my days filled with the laughter of my children, Sophie and Lucas, and dreams shared with my husband, Blake, until his untimely heart failure.

Despite my savvy, Alex Jennings—then Drew Coleman—had completely charmed me, his romance scam leaving a deep, searing sting of betrayal. A bitter reminder of my vulnerability at that time. Yet, it wasn't just about feeling duped; it was about recognizing the deep loneliness and craving for connection that had made me the perfect target. Drew had expertly exploited a need in me that I hadn't fully acknowledged to myself.

Drew was a facade, a mirage. A master scammer, he left devastation in his wake, preying on those blinded by wealth and love. I was just another notch on his belt, my life and legacy nearly erased by his greed. The car crash? No accident; it was an assassination attempt that snatched the lives of my beautiful children, Sophie and Lucas, and left me in darkness for six long months. Coming out of the coma, I was forced to navigate the depths of grief and despair alone.

Why didn't he finish the job? Maybe he underestimated a broken woman's resolve to rise again.

Big mistake.

SEVEN WAYS TO BURY A MAN

It was during those long, grueling hours in physical therapy, as I relearned to walk and regain control over my shattered body, that I plotted my revenge. In a dusty, dog-eared notebook hidden beneath my rehabilitation tools, I began to draft my manifesto—'Seven Ways to Bury a Man.' Each chapter outlined a strategy to dismantle Alex, piece by piece until nothing of the man I hated remained.

1 Surveillance and Investigation—Learn his habits and track his movements to use them against him.
2 Digital Manipulation—Create a network of lies to ensnare him.
3 Public Exposure—Reveal his deceit in the most humiliating way possible.
4 Physical Confrontation—Confront him, and let him see the face of his downfall.
5 Emotional Confrontation—Force him to face the emotional devastation he created.
6 Assassination—The culmination of my plans, the ultimate retribution.
7 Psychological Closure—Burying him and our past, allowing me to move on.

As these strategies crystallized, each session of pain and rehabilitation fused them deeper into my psyche. They became my silent creed, my unwavering path to salvation. Drew's betrayal killed Audrey Moore, and with her, the loving mother of Sophie and Lucas. Their laughter and play, once the heartbeat of my days, now echoed as silent grief.

From those ashes rose Veronica Kane, reborn with a relentless drive for payback. New name, new hair, same old disdain for scammers with charming smiles.

The distant wail of a police siren suddenly pierced the air, an abrupt reminder of the world outside. It was just a patrol car passing by, its presence fleeting as it moved on to distant urgencies, but it snapped me back to the reality of my current mission. I'd spent all week laying the groundwork for the next stage of my plan, planting seeds of doubt about the bastard. Emails, seeming to come from concerned friends, landed in the right inboxes. Social media became a battleground of half-truths and outright lies about Alex. The ensuing uproar marked the beginning of his undoing, a carefully orchestrated symphony of digital whispers and doubts.

I had recently learned of Alex and Carrie's engagement party, and as the day drew near, the significance of this event for my agenda crystallized. It wasn't just a social gathering; it became the stage for my final act to expose him. This gathering, set against a backdrop of opulence and false pretenses, would be where I'd strip away his veneer of respectability in front of those he'd deceived most.

My infiltration was already in motion. Anticipation and a hunger for justice, each magnifying the other, fueled my drive to ruin the man who thought he could outrun his past. As the festivities and the climax of my plan neared, a familiar ache in my head tested my resolve, the throbbing a stark reminder of the crash meant to end me.

But now, I would end him.

The silence in my hotel room was heavy, like a blanket too thick for the season. I sat on the edge of the bed, the only light casting long shadows that seemed to stretch further with every passing minute. Alone, I couldn't escape the voices of my past therapy sessions. They seemed louder in the quiet.

For two years, I dove into the depths of grief and anger in therapy. I could still hear Dr. Adler's voice, "Letting go is not forgetting," a mantra aimed at guiding me through my heartache. "It's about forgiveness, about choosing the path forward."

But forgiveness felt like a betrayal—not just of my lost loved ones, but of the person I'd become. My therapist pushed for peace, for reconciliation with my past. Yet, I was grateful for the relentless pursuit of payback. It pulled me back from the edge, gave me purpose when I had none. Adler's sessions, meant to heal, only seemed to enhance my focus. In the shadows of our conversations, I discovered not peace, but a steely clarity.

As I ruminated on this, a sharp knock at my hotel door interrupted the steady patter of rain on the window. Glancing at the clock, I noted it was too late for visitors, but just in time for a last-minute delivery. I wasn't expecting company, but I was expecting a package. Opening the door, I found a drenched delivery person, wearing a rain jacket with the hood pulled back, revealing a faded T-shirt of The Killers, the distinctive neon-lit logo still vibrant despite the wear.

For a fleeting moment, I was transported back to a summer

night years ago, under the open sky filled with stars and the echoes of "Mr. Brightside" filling the air. I remembered how the crowd sang along to every word, their voices rising in a chorus of bittersweet euphoria. It had been a carefree night, one of many that now seemed like fragments of another life—life before deception and darkness had taken hold.

"Veronica Kane?" The delivery person's voice was muffled by a sudden increase in the downpour.

"I'm Veronica," I replied, taking the box and signing on the digital pad with my well-practiced alias name. He gave a barely perceptible nod, then slipped back into the storm, as silent and swift as a shadow.

Back inside, I turned the box over in my hands. This was it—the final piece of my plan. Inside were the high-grade listening devices I'd ordered, small enough to be overlooked, powerful enough to capture every whisper at the engagement party. It was a gamble, but what part of my scheme wasn't? Setting the box aside, I poured a glass of whiskey, letting the gravity of tomorrow's undertaking wash over me. This wasn't just preparation; it was the eve of battle.

My temporary living space, now cluttered with the tools of my mission, felt more like a war room. The glow from multiple laptop screens illuminated the dark, casting long shadows against the walls. They flickered with the endless scroll of social media feeds, burner phones, surveillance footage, and drafts of emails—each a piece of the intricate web I'd weaved.

The campaign was tearing through social media, with rumors of Alex's dodgy finances and shady ethics gaining traction among the online crowd. I watched as screens filled with data showed my manufactured concerns turning into hot topics. Every tweet and post was a deliberate stroke in the broader strategy—set up to create maximum impact at the engagement party. I'd prepared those closest to him for an upheaval that was yet to be unveiled.

I reached for another whiskey, its amber liquid reflecting the artificial light, and knocked it back hard, followed by another. Stress has a way of dragging back old habits; the ashtray full of butts next to me was proof enough. Each drag was a brief escape; each exhale, a mix of tension and resolve.

Rain drummed against the window, pulling my thoughts from the screens. It reminded me of another day, one soaked in rain, when I'd forgotten my umbrella and stood resigned to getting drenched. That's when Drew showed up, holding the sunflower-patterned umbrella I'd left behind. It was more than shelter; it felt like a beam of light on a dark day. "Thought you might need this," he'd said, flipping it open over us both. The closeness of the moment made my heart jump. "Can't have you catching a cold, can we?"

My response was a jumble, caught between surprise and gratitude, marveling at how in tune he was with my needs. We walked under that shared umbrella, the city around us melting into a rain-blurred dream. I thanked him, our lips meeting briefly in a tender kiss.

"Of course," he'd said, his voice blending with the rain—a gentle reminder of his thoughtfulness. That stroll under the umbrella felt otherworldly, every detail vivid, each moment amplified by the downpour. Drew had a way of making me feel noticed, understood, and safe.

Now, the rhythm of the rain outside played a melancholic tune, echoing a life once lived. I yearned for the simplicity of those times, for the version of myself who believed in the beauty of random acts of kindness. Yet, that memory, bright as it was, served as a milestone of everything I had lost, and how far down the path of vengeance I had come.

With a heavy heart, I turned my attention back to the screens. Tomorrow was the engagement party. The day of Alex's judgment.

The engagement party was alive with anticipation and cheer, a vivid counterpoint to the chilling resolve I felt. I was undercover as one of the event staff, having cobbled together a uniform online—it was a typical event outfit: crisp white shirt paired with black slacks, nothing that screamed for attention.

A bit of digital maneuvering got me on the event management company's roster. The cover story was straightforward and effective: I was filling in for a staff member who had a sudden family emergency, a person who wouldn't be missed.

As I stood in front of the bathroom mirror, adjusting the uniform that was now my shield, I was acutely aware of the choices I had made to accommodate my physical limitations. The flat, sensible shoes were a deliberate decision, a nod to the limp I needed to mask. They weren't as stylish as the heels other women wore, but they let me move with a grace that disguised the pain I felt.

To ensure I remained a ghost to Alex, the only person who could blow my cover, I had transformed myself. The wig, with its auburn curls, was a far cry from my usual straight blonde hair, and a pair of glasses subtly altered my face.

As I took in the room, I noticed the crowd was less than you'd expect for such a big event. My campaign of digital whispers had helped thin the ranks of guests. Fewer faces meant fewer distractions, and those who mattered most were still present. In some ways, the reduced numbers worked to my advantage, making my surveillance and maneuvering through the crowd easier and less obstructed. However, I also couldn't help feeling a little exposed, despite my disguise.

As a few more stragglers entered the venue, the air became thick with perfume and the din of conversations. I moved about unnoticed, my tasks as a staff member merely a front as I monitored the celebration's flow and awaited the right moment.

Just then, Miranda, the event coordinator, a sharp-eyed woman with an unmistakable air of authority, approached me abruptly. "You! There's a spill near Table 12. Handle it," she commanded, pointing briskly towards a crowded section of the hall. I had once fantasized about a glamorous undercover role. Now here I was, the reluctant star of the spill cleanup crew.

I nodded and turned to grab the necessary cleaning supplies when her voice cut through again, "And hurry, God forbid, we have a guest slip on the floor. What's your name again?"

The question caught me off guard. "Gi—Gina," I replied quickly. My hesitation made her eyes narrow suspiciously. Her gaze drilled into my back as I walked away, a knot of anxiety tightening in my stomach. This was a wake-up call. Despite all my meticulous planning, everything could unravel at any moment.

I cleaned the mess quickly, focusing intently on the task, and returned to my surveillance duties, still rattled from my encounter with Miranda. It was clear I needed to blend in better, just another face in the crowd, and be seen to be doing my supposed job. I picked up a tray, loaded it with canapes, and wandered through the crowd.

Once I felt sufficiently inconspicuous, I stole a moment to

check the compact projector I'd smuggled in and hidden in a discreet corner. All around me, the guests, adorned in their finest, remained blissfully ignorant of the drama about to unfold. Carrie and Alex, the epitome of a perfect couple, floated through the evening, symbols of a future I was about to dismantle.

I monitored the room with the sophisticated listening devices that had arrived at my hotel the night before. High-grade microphones, tiny yet powerful, were strategically placed around the venue, each linked to an app on my phone. With a discreet tap, I skipped from one hushed accusation to another, my app lighting up with icons that represented different microphones around the room. I paused on a particularly juicy revelation about Alex's past ventures, the voices clear and condemning.

This was the evidence I needed, proof that my digital tendrils had entwined effectively around Alex's neck. "You hear about that business in Australia? Pretty dicey," one guest murmured, casting a wary glance at Alex. *Dicey was an understatement*, I thought, a grim satisfaction curling inside me as I remembered the carefully crafted emails hinting at suspicious dealings I had seeded among Alex's contacts.

As I moved through the clusters of elegantly dressed guests, whispers fluttered around me like leaves in a storm—hints of hidden gambling debts, secretive late-night escapades, and abrupt business failures. Each snippet added to the cacophony, a symphony of doubt and suspicion that swirled through the opulently appointed room.

"It's weird that he travels so much," one curious voice stated through the buzz. It echoed in my mind, pulling me back to those nights when Alex—or rather Drew—had often canceled our plans at the last minute, claiming an urgent business trip. So obvious now, in retrospect. His constant travels were fabrications designed to cover his tracks.

Across the room, a cluster of women murmured behind their hands, eyes darting towards Alex as they did. One shook her head slightly, the confusion evident on her face as she digested a rumor about Alex's mysterious past. I watched as doubt took root; the visual unrest as compelling as the whispers themselves.

Even the congratulations to the guests of honor I overheard seemed tinged with a hint of reservation as if each well-wisher weighed the sincerity of their words against the rumors they'd absorbed. This subtle shift in perception was exactly what I'd aimed for—injecting just enough suspicion to make the crowd receptive to the doubts I was about to confirm on a larger scale. As I listened, I felt a grim satisfaction; the seeds of doubt were sprouting just as the peak of the evening approached.

Before the moment we all awaited, close friends took the stage, sharing rehearsed anecdotes, sketching a picture of two lives woven tightly together. Beneath the occasional laughter and applause, however, a subtle tension hummed—evidence of the doubts I had seeded among Alex's circle.

It was against this backdrop of humorous tales and hidden skepticism that Carrie and Alex rose to speak—the pinnacle of the evening. The celebration so far had painted a portrait of a couple destined for a shared future, a portrait I was poised to shred.

As the engagement party swirled around me, a headache, thunderous and demanding, chose that moment to declare its presence, gnawing at the edges of my focus. It was a migraine, a familiar torment since the accident, squeezing my temples mercilessly. For a brief moment, the pain peaked, and I stumbled slightly, my vision blurring. I managed to place my tray on a nearby table without dropping it. A nearby guest, a tall man with a neatly trimmed beard and a concerned expression, reached out, steadying me with a gentle hand on my elbow. 'Are you alright?' he murmured, his voice a distant echo through the pain.

"Just a bit dizzy, thank you," I mumbled, managing a weak smile as I steadied myself. I groped in my slacks' pockets, seeking the small bottle of pills I usually kept handy. But it wasn't there— lost in the rush of preparations. Lately, my diligence with my medications had slipped, a dangerous oversight.

"When I met Alex," Carrie began, "I found not just a partner, but a soulmate. Our journey through Italy, Greece, and France wasn't just a trip—it was the beginning of our beautiful future together." With every word, she drew smiles and nods from the audience. Yet, the murmurs I caught through my listening devices hinted at the crowd's hesitance, their whispers clashing with the public displays of affection.

It was against this backdrop of shared stories and laughter that I executed my plan. While the official slideshow—filled with dates and places marking their love story—began its narration on the main screen, I initiated a shadow play of my own making.

I shook off the unease that permeated me and zeroed in on my mission. Everything was set. No turning back. My fingers clenched around the remote for the projector, grounding me in spite of the continued throbbing pain in my head.

On the stage, Carrie continued, "Every moment with Alex is a chapter in the most beautiful story we're writing together. Whether it's laughing under the Tuscan sun, dancing in the streets of Santorini, or walking hand in hand along the Seine, every experience has been filled with the magic of discovery—not just of the places we visited but of each other."

She paused, a tender smile playing on her lips as she looked over at Alex. "He teaches me, challenges me. This engagement isn't just a promise for a wedding; it's a vow to continue exploring life together, to support and cherish each other through every high and every low."

She finished with a toast, "To love, laughter, and happily ever after," her eyes locked with Alex's. There was applause, of course, yet the claps were tempered by the whispered doubts that now circulated more openly, spurred by the groundwork I had laid.

The room's anticipation shifted to Alex. He stepped up, the very embodiment of confidence, as was his stock in trade. Taking the microphone, his voice filled the space with a resonant warmth. His hand reached out and found Carrie's as he spoke. "Standing here with Carrie, I'm reminded of the incredible journey that has led us to this moment," he began. "She has become my guiding light. Her strength, her grace, and her unwavering love have transformed me in ways I could never have imagined."

He paused, allowing his words to sink in, his gaze never straying from Carrie. "Our travels were more than escapades; they were a journey of the heart. These memories you're about to see projected, they're not just souvenirs; they're the foundation on which we build our future."

Alex raised his glass. "To Carrie, my everything." The room, once again, offered their approval and looks of conflicted admiration—applause laced with the residue of skepticism, echoing the duality of their feelings toward the couple.

Alex gave a nod, cueing an event employee to kick off the slideshow. The opening frames, each stamped with dates and exotic locales like "Paris, February 25, 2024," and "Istanbul, May 12, 2024," drew the audience deeper into a narrative spun from love and laughter, depicting Alex and Carrie in snapshots of sheer joy.

Tucked away in a discreet corner of the venue, my setup lay hidden: a laptop wired to a small but powerful projector I had managed to smuggle inside. A press of the remote, and another wall lit up with my own selection of images, offering a stark contrast to the idyllic scenes playing out on the main screen. As these competing narratives unfolded across the room, a wave of confusion rippled through the assembled guests. Heads turned and eyes darted between the two displays as the crowd grappled with the clashing versions of reality laid before them.

My first slide flashed "Aspen, Colorado, March 10, 2024." This date, buried deep within the timeline of Alex and Carrie's relationship, set the stage for the emergence of Alex's affair with Anya, the naïve Russian model whose dreams of runway stardom had led her into a far more compromising reality. The explicit image that followed snapped the crowd to attention. It left no room for innocent interpretations, their intimacy both undeniable and raw.

The initial shock quickly morphed into outrage as the slideshow peeled back the layers of Alex's deception. Whispers escalated to gasps and then to voices thick with indignation. Questions and accusations flew, slicing through the air as the audience grappled with the visceral truth.

As each new timestamp unfolded, revealing further indiscretions—"Beverly Hills, CA, April 5, 2024," followed by "Malibu, CA, May 22, 2024"—the contrast between Alex's portrayed commitment to Carrie and his clandestine actions became undeniable.

The room plunged into turmoil, and I watched, a deep satisfaction settling in me. The evidence of his deceit was undeniable, laid bare for all to see. I couldn't help but tune into the reactions of the crowd through my earpiece connected to the listening devices around the venue. Each gasp of shock, each muttered condemnation, played to me like a symphony—the symphony of Alex's downfall.

The atmosphere in the room shifted instantly from warmth and jubilation to a cold, palpable horror. Carrie, struck by betrayal, stood frozen as the damning evidence of Alex's infidelity emerged before her. Alex, caught like a deer in headlights, fumbled for words that refused to come. It was almost disappointing; I had expected better ad-libbing from such a professional fabulist.

The justice I had pursued for so long was unfurling before my eyes, yet the sight of Carrie's anguish tempered my triumph. She was collateral damage in a war she hadn't chosen, her dreams publicly shattered in the most humiliating way.

As the scandalous photos continued to flash across the screen, murmurs grew into a tempest of voices. Suddenly, a sudden movement sliced through the chaos. Carrie's brother, Tommy, driven by a mix of protective fury and disbelief, charged through the crowd toward Alex, his expression etched with rage.

Alex!" he roared, his voice cutting through the commotion. The room fell into a stunned silence, every eye fixed on the developing drama.

Before anyone could intervene, Tommy's fist crashed into Alex's jaw, sending him reeling backward. The sound of the blow was crisp and brutal, a physical expression of the betrayal exposed for all to see. Alex clutched his face, a mix of shock and pain written across his features as he staggered, trying to find his footing.

Carrie's face was a canvas of shock and anguish as she cried out, "Stop it! Just stop!" Yet her plea was swallowed by the sudden tumult that erupted following the punch. The room surged into a frenzy, some guests pushing forward to intervene, others merely spectators drawn to the unfolding drama. In the chaotic aftermath of the punch, some guests clustered around Carrie, guiding her away from the turmoil, while others formed a human barrier between Alex and any further attacks. The air was thick with commotion, a clamorous blend of condemnation, sympathy, and outright disbelief.

Alex, cradling his jaw, his earlier poise in ruins, scanned the room. The faces of friends and family now looked back at him in horror and distrust. The veneer of the perfect fiancé had cracked and was now totally shattered, the deceit beneath laid bare for all to see.

From my vantage point on the sidelines, I observed the scene with mixed emotions. The physical confrontation had heightened the impact of the evening's revelations, sparking a blaze of reactions that words alone could not have kindled. As I slipped away into the rainy night, the echoes of the engagement party's collapse rang in my ears.

SEVEN WAYS TO BURY A MAN

Amid the turmoil, a bitter satisfaction filled me—I had liberated Carrie from a future built on lies. My extreme measures, though harsh, had prevented her from sharing my fate.

The headache, relentless since it began, had ratcheted up. It was a physical reflection of the night's escalating stress. As the chaos peaked around me, the throbbing in my head pounded in sync, underscoring the fragility I continually fought to hide.

My objective had been clear: expose Alex and drag the truth into the light. Yet, as I made my way through the shadows of the city, the final part of my plan awaited enactment, a final confrontation that loomed dark and inevitable.

The simple lock on Alex's back door was a joke—a testament to his arrogance, his belief that he was beyond reach, untouchable. Now, as I sat hidden in the shadows of his living room, I was the predator silently waiting in another predator's den. Beside me, the cold, hard presence of a baseball bat lay within easy reach. Its weight was a grim harbinger of what was to come. Its partner, a gun, lay silently in my lap, offering cold reassurance. The weak spill of streetlight barely cut through the room's darkness.

The throbbing in my head had grown from a distressing hindrance to an all-consuming migraine, syncing painfully with my heartbeat. "Should've gone back for my meds," I chastised myself, the irony biting. Here I was, preparing to confront the man I blamed for my world's unraveling, yet I had neglected the one thing that kept my physical unraveling at bay.

The sound of the key turning in the lock snapped me back to the present, a jolt of adrenaline slicing through the fog of pain. My grip on the bat tightened. As the door swung open and Alex stepped into the dimly lit room, the world seemed to hold its breath.

I watched. A shadow among shadows.

His silhouette sharpened into focus. I struck, delivering my own brutal critique of his performance that evening. The bat, an extension of my will, connected with the back of his head—not enough to knock him out, but enough to stun him. He staggered, his hand clutching the impact site. Then, a muffled groan escaped his lips as he collapsed to the floor.

My movements were swift and practiced—the result of countless mental rehearsals.

Before he could find his bearings, I had him tied up. Tying another human shook me—researching it was one thing, doing it was another. I placed a chair just out of his reach, a quiet assertion of control, and then melted back into the shadows.

"Surprise, Alex," I said, my voice steady despite the tempest inside me. "Bet you didn't see this coming in your bogus forecasts."

The stillness was heavy, charged with the weight of a thousand deceits. On the floor, Alex moaned, his movements sluggish and disjointed as he tried to grasp his predicament.

"A lot of drama to get here, I admit," I continued. "But you and I need to talk."

The dim glow barely illuminated his face, contorted with confusion and pain as he wrestled against the ropes, his efforts disoriented and weak. I leaned forward slightly, letting the scant light sketch my face into the gloom. "You might remember a certain fiasco at a certain engagement party recently."

Alex squinted into the darkness, trying to locate me, but I stayed cloaked in shadow. "I orchestrated that, Alex, just like this," I said, my voice even but tinged with satisfaction. "I'm in control."

I paused, letting the weight of my words sink in. Shadows deepened, signaling more revelations to come. He strained against the dark, his frustration clear as he failed to see my face.

His voice cracked with confusion, "Why. . .why would you do this? Why go through all this just to expose my affair?" His incredulity was raw, his vulnerability exposed in each word.

He struggled harder against his bonds, the ropes biting into his wrists as he tried to rise, desperate for a better view of me, or perhaps to locate an escape route. His bewilderment was evident, his writhing chaotic as he tried to make sense of the ruins of his engagement party.

"'*Just* an affair,'" I snapped at him, the bitterness unmistakable. A spike of pain jolted through my skull. I pressed a hand to my throbbing temple, steadying myself. Memories flashed before me—the simple joy of our first shared coffee on a chilly morning, him warming my hands with his, a gesture that promised so much more. A visceral reminder of what had led me here. The irony wasn't lost on me—here I was, unveiling truths while battling to keep my own world from unraveling.

"Cruelty and deception," I said, my voice cold. "Is that how you see the world?" His face, barely visible in the shadows, showed him grappling to comprehend. "Do you even recognize the harm you cause, or have you convinced yourself that this is how the world operates? Maybe to you, everyone is just an obstacle."

I let the quiet deepen, my grip on the gun tightening. "You need to see the consequences of your actions. They extend far beyond what you choose to see."

His discomfort was clear; his usual semblance of control was failing. "Who. . .are you?" he asked, his voice tinged with pain and fear.

The question struck a nerve. "Who am I?" I said, feeling the absurdity of his question reverberating in my head, a bad joke. "I'm the ghost you forgot about."

He continued to feign ignorance. "Look, I don't know what you want. If it's money—"

"Money?" I scoffed. With a swift motion fueled by years of pent-up rage, I knelt and grabbed him by the collar, pressing the gun firmly against his temple. He froze, his eyes wide with the fear of a man staring down the barrel of dawning consequences.

"Let's clarify," my voice was low, menacing. "This isn't about money. It's a classic story—boy meets girl, boy loses girl, boy tries to kill the girl. But this time, the girl becomes the hero of her own story."

He squirmed as I moved the gun across his throat, cutting off his words.

"Remember poor Audrey Moore?" I said deliberately, each word heavy with significance. "A successful entrepreneur, a mother, a widow—you thought she was an easy mark in 2021."

His panic was palpable, each truth I revealed tightening the noose.

"Along came this snake, Drew Coleman. He slithered into her life, spinning stories of future wealth. He executed the long con—offering love, playing the perfect partner. All of it complete and total bullshit."

A sharp pain lanced through my head, but adrenaline drove me on. 'He didn't just deceive; he took everything—her heart, her trust, her financial security. And when he'd drained her, he orchestrated a car crash intended to kill her and her children—erasing her entire legacy." The weight of my words filled the room, heavy with the gravity of truth.

"And when the wreckage settled, this man, Drew Coleman,

vanished, shedding his skin to emerge as Alex Jennings. To prey on others, such as Carrie Bristol."

The room absorbed the weight of my words, charged with unalloyed truth.

I paused, letting the magnitude of my accusations press down on him, the gun steady in my grip. "This isn't about revenge, lover. It's about justice. It's about stopping you from destroying more lives."

As I spoke, I reached up, pulled off the wig that concealed me, and let my blonde hair fall around my shoulders. The face he once loved was exposed as my glasses hit the floor with a clatter. My gaze drilled into his. Unyielding.

"You asked me why I'd go through all this trouble?" My grip tightened on his collar, as firm as the gun in my hand. "Because I'm the one you couldn't break, asshole. And I'm here to make sure you don't destroy another life like you did mine."

Alex met my eyes, his face trembling. "Now you listen to me. I've made mistakes, I've hurt people. I don't deny that," he pleaded, his voice tinged with frustration and an attempt at reason. "But murder? Conspiring to kill children? That's insanity. I don't know who you are or what the hell you're talking about!"

His denials came quickly, his pleas persuasive. He was a master at convincing. A vivid memory interrupted my thoughts— the laughter and clinking glasses from a summer evening when we celebrated another round of funding my tech startup had secured.

Drew was there, his smile broad, his hand light on the small of my back, whispering promises of forever into my ear. That night, under the backyard's soft string lights, the air was alive with talk of my company's potential. I believed in him utterly, in our shared future.

The contrast between that joyful memory and the grim reality in front of me sharpened the sting. The man before me now, bound and frightened, seemed a shadow of the one in my memory. Was any part of that warmth real, or was it all just a part of his con?

For two years, one question had haunted me, echoing relentlessly. My hunt for Alex was more than a quest for justice, I wanted an answer to the only question that truly mattered. I leaned closer, the gun still pressed against his temple.

"Did you ever love me, Drew?"

The question lingered, thick with meaning. His silence was infuriating, but his puzzled look threw me.

"Even a little?" I pressed, hating the exposure of my

vulnerability. The words, once spoken, seemed to take on a life of their own.

His eyes widened, not with fear, but with confusion. "Love? Lady, I don't even know who you are," he stammered, his expression softening—regret or another deceit?

The room seemed to tilt as his words hit me, the torment in my head rising to an unbearable crescendo. My grip on the gun faltered, and my hands trembled.

He faced me, his voice raw. "Please, listen, OK? I'm not who you think I am. Yes, I had an affair, but everything else you've accused me of is not true, you've got the wrong guy."

His tone was unsettling, almost convincing.

"Look at this. . .look here. . ." he struggled slightly, turning his arm to show the inside of his bicep where a faded tattoo was visible. "You see that?" It was a U.S. Marine Corps emblem, with the initials 'A.J.' and a service number beneath it, the ink blurred by time but the meaning unmistakable.

"A.J. stands for Alex Jennings; I got this in the military right out of high school."

The tattoo made me hesitate. It wasn't conclusive proof—there could be explanations—but it sowed seeds of doubt, undermining the certainty I had held so tightly. His bewildered demeanor further chipped away at the story I had believed.

God help me if I was wrong.

A renewed surge of pain shot through my head, intensifying the inner chaos. My hands trembled, the gun's cold metal nearly slipping from my grip. I pressed my palms to my temples, struggling to keep my crumbling thoughts intact.

Sensing my hesitation, Alex's instincts seemed to kick in. With a desperate grunt, he lunged at me, his movements fueled by fear and a desperate will to live.

Motion blurred. Sounds muffled. Then, the gun's sharp report. Alex's body jerked from the impact, his face contorting with shock and agony before he stumbled and fell heavily. Seeing him so vulnerable, so starkly human, cut through my rage.

I dropped the gun; its clatter resonated in the hushed room. My breathing was ragged, each breath a tangled amalgam of relief and despair. As I sank to my knees, the room spun, shadows merging into a disorienting swirl.

Alex lay gasping, clutching his abdomen where the bullet had hit. Instinctively, I reached out to press against the wound, trying futilely to stem the bleeding. Looking into his eyes—eyes devoid of any recognition of me or my torment—I faced the harsh truth.

This man wasn't Drew.

The realization hit like a gut punch; my actions were irreversible. Recoiling, I withdrew my blood-soaked hands, the room growing colder, and the shadows deepening. All that remained was a silent reverberation of my question, haunting and unanswered: "Did you ever love me?" It was more than just about him. It was about every choice and every delusion that had led me to this moment.

As the gunshot's echo faded, I froze. My first instinct was to call 911, to get help quickly. I pulled my phone from my jacket and hesitated over the call button, but then I saw the man's still form. He was motionless, no longer in agony. Only a deep, unsettling stillness remained.

A wave of despair washed over me. Calling an ambulance was pointless now. A chilling thought followed—was I ready to face prison? To pay for my actions?

As these thoughts swirled about my mind, I noticed the blinking light on my phone—the voicemail indicator flashing insistently. A glaring beacon of the world beyond this dark, tragic room. I pressed the voicemail button, hands still shaking, and the phone brought up 28 unheard messages. The most recent one played automatically, my psychiatrist's voice cutting through the silence, fraught with concern.

"This is Dr. Adler. . .again. Please call me back immediately. I'm very concerned that you haven't refilled your meds. Let's review your treatment plan immediately and make sure we're preventing any escalation of symptoms. Thank you."

I shoved the phone into my pocket after reviewing several more voicemails from Adler, the same reductive message over and over again. Her world, neatly ordered by dosages and therapy sessions, was too constrained, too clinical. She saw my actions through the lens of schizoaffective disorder and PTSD—labels that were supposed to explain everything but explained nothing about the raw, human need for justice.

I'm more than just Adler's diagnosis, and I'm sure as hell more than the surgeon's prognosis of brain damage. These terms don't capture the entirety of who I have become. They don't explain the depth of pain or the burning need for resolution that has driven me to this point. Adler's treatments, aimed at numbing the symptoms, couldn't numb the memories or the drive within me.

When doctors look at me, all they see is a patient. But I see a world they've never known, a pain they've never felt. Adler's approach feels shallow at times—pills and therapy sessions simply checkboxes on a form. They help. Maybe? But they also don't reach the deep places. Where the real anguish lives. Some wounds are woven into the fabric of who I am. Until doctors can offer something that truly speaks to that, their prescriptions will remain just another unchecked box in my life.

As I switch off my phone, the stillness of the room is suddenly broken by another sound—distant at first, then growing steadily louder: the unmistakable wail of sirens. A jolt of adrenaline surges through me. A reminder that the world outside hasn't stopped moving, even as my own seems to have frozen in time.

The realization that the gunshot might have been heard by someone nearby gets me moving. The sirens are real—not illusions, not tricks of my troubled mind.

No time for regret. The need to act, to decide my next move, consumes me. I glance at Alex's lifeless body, feeling the weight of my actions. The wail of sirens snaps me back again to the present. After a quick sweep for any incriminating evidence, I slip out the back door, disappearing into the night.

The cold air strikes me hard as I burst outside, chilling me through my clothes. Each breath is sharp. The ground beneath my feet feels unstable as if I'm running through a dream, each step heavy and uncertain.

I run, driven by survival, my thoughts racing: Where to go? What to do? Is there any escape? The sirens grow louder, in discordant syncopation, with my heartbeat.

Despite my limp, I press on, haunted by memories of my lost children, of my old life.

Rounding a corner, a streetlamp's glare blinds me momentarily. I stumble, brace myself against a rough brick wall, the scrape of it rough against my palms.

I push off and keep running. The city feels like a prison, a maze. Part of me wants to stop, surrender, and let the end come. But another part, the fighter Drew woke in me, keeps me moving.

The sirens fade, their cries dimming, as I distance myself from the scene. The pounding in my head subsides, replaced by cold clarity. I'm free for the moment, but the freedom tastes like ash. I'm not just running from the police; I'm running from the reality of who I've become.

The chill in the air is more than the night. An all-too-familiar ache troubles the base of my skull, reminding me of deeper wounds. Drew Coleman—that name. It triggers a dark drive within me to hunt him down, again and again.

But then, a flash of cruel lucidity cuts through—the night I drove drunk. The humiliation of being taken for a ride in a romance scam. The despair of being left behind by Drew like yesterday's trash. The loneliness I felt after. It was all too much.

The crash—it was all my doing. My kids died because of my drunk actions, not Drew's manipulations. Dr. Adler says my mind rewrote the story to make it into a more acceptable narrative. She says I cast Drew as the villain to mask my own guilt. It was easier to chase a monster than face the truth.

A cascade of images then. The glazed look in Drew's eyes as he stared up from the asphalt. Smoke rising from the barrel of my gun as I watched him bleed out. I tracked him down and killed him well over a year ago. Before him, there were others—each one a face mistaken for Drew's in the dim light of my grief and anger. Their expressions frozen in shock, not understanding why.

As I blend into the shadows of the city, the realization that this cycle is far from broken seeps into me. My steps are quick but aimless, guided by a swirling chaos that retakes its place in my thoughts. It propels me forward into the night.

Drew must pay.

Behind me, the far-off sirens reach their zenith, likely converging on Alex's home. But the police, the sirens, the consequences—they all seem part of another world. For me, there's only the hunt, the relentless pursuit of a ghost.

The pounding headache fades completely, and with it comes a certain calmness. Drew Coleman beckons me onward. And I follow, because what else is there?

In the cold embrace of the night, I disappear into the city's forgotten lanes. As the sirens dwindle into the distance, replaced by the haunting echoes of my own footsteps, I realize the true horror isn't that I might continue to seek Drew Coleman—it's that I can never stop.

THE PAINTED UNSEEN

THE WORLD WAS like an unraveling tapestry of horrors en route to Ava Tarlow's estate. Madness gripped the city. Innocents had become vessels of chaos, running through the streets.

"The world is going to hell," Sebastian offered as Margot Havelock maneuvered her '69 Boss Mustang through the pandemonium. "But at least the damn rain has stopped."

Margot, a striking figure exuding elegance and confidence, had raven-black hair that framed her face with mystery. Her unwavering determination shone through piercing emerald-green eyes. Adorned in a tailored black coat with concealed pockets for occult tools, she wore intricate silver jewelry symbolizing protection and power.

Sebastian, once a nobleman from ancient York, was now Margot's spectral partner, irrevocably cursed into the form of a midnight blue cat. He sat poised and alert on the passenger seat.

Moments later, Ava's Victorian mansion emerged through a dense mist, a majestic relic amidst the modern world. It displayed an ornate facade with intricate carvings and stained-glass windows. The reclusive artist hadn't answered her phone for several days, and though Sebastian sensed her inside, she couldn't or wouldn't answer the door.

The city was in mayhem thanks to Ava's sorcerous artwork, leaving no time for subtlety. Margot picked the front door lock, as Sebastian marveled at the estate's enormity. "Tsk tsk. All this fame and fortune, yet you claim Ava has no artistic talent?"

Margot continued working the lock. "Well, let's just say she's like Picasso. . .if Picasso forgot how to paint. It's her cursed paintbrush that holds all the talent.

Sebastian paced. "This 'Brush of Whispers' is. . .fascinating. Did she tell you how she came upon it?"

Margot grimaced with frustration at the lock. "Said she found it in a half-buried chest in the mansion's cellar. Inherited this place from her uncle, who was an artist as well. Guy went bonkers and died in a booby hatch."

"I believe they're called psychiatric hospitals these days, dear."

"Whatever."

"What did she hope for you to achieve, anyway?" Sebastian mused aloud.

The lock clicked. Margo opened the door. "Simple. She wanted to keep the prestige and wealth the brush offered but lose its curse. Clearly, the brush has other plans."

As they entered the darkened foyer, Margot unconsciously grasped the hilt of Nightfire—an enchanted sword adorning her hip and one of many weapons she kept in her car trunk.

Beyond the foyer and Grand Hall, passageways seemed to stretch endlessly, twisting like a labyrinth. Moonlight cast eerie shadows across Ava's grotesque artwork, depicting nightmarish creatures. The air felt heavy, the scent foul.

Without warning, Margot and Sebastian were violently yanked to the floor and pinned down by an invisible force. The power was undeniable, as if reality itself strained under an unseen weight.

⫸⫸⫸⫷⫷⫷

Hours earlier, Margot had stood amidst the shadows of the Midnight Curiosities shop, studying an ancient painting. It held the key to deciphering the horrors plaguing her client, Ava Tarlow, and might save a city teetering on the edge of anarchy.

The nameless artwork embodied morbid curiosity, enticing viewers with body parts, symbolic fragments, and a profound sense of disquiet. It laid bare veiled confessions and dark secrets on canvas.

Margot brushed rainwater from her cheek, the storm still raging outside. The proprietor, Victor Blackwood, who lived on the top floor, had reluctantly opened his establishment in the dead of night, convinced by Margot's serious demeanor.

He then scurried off to make hot tea, anticipating a long night.

"Deciphered it yet?" Margot asked, fully aware that the room was not as empty as it appeared.

Sebastian, choosing to remain magically unseen except to Margot, leapt onto a nearby table, tail swishing inquisitively. Ignoring her, he leisurely licked his left hind leg.

Margot sighed in resignation. "Please. . .OK?" she said through gritted teeth.

Sebastian grinned with feline satisfaction. "Better. A glimmer of appreciation for my linguistic expertise."

Margo glared back.

Sebastian licked himself twice, then glanced at the painting. "The signature on that atrocity is a forgotten Mayan script—*Buluc-Chabtan Ucan*. *Buluc-Chabtan* is a feared death god, and '*Ucan*' means 'noble Mayan family.' Likely a nom de guerre."

"I know that name."

Victor's distinguished voice startled Margot and Sebastian as he appeared with a tray of steaming tea.

Margot nodded. "Then let's talk."

Margot strained against the arcane energy that had pinned her and Sebastian to the mansion's floor. "Are you okay?" she called out.

Sebastian yowled in frustration. "What's the point of being a magical companion if I can't conjure my way out of magical restraints!"

Ava Tarlow—or what remained of her—emerged from the shadows, defying gravity as she clung to the high ceiling. Her contorted body sprouted spider-like limbs and menacing sharp claws.

"I know why you're here, witch," said the possessing entity, its voice like a thousand whispers intertwined. "And I've faced your kind before."

It descended farther on a thread that emerged from its back. Its grotesque features became discernible—a fusion of the known and the unknowable. "Even if Ava were in control, she would never acquiesce to the plan we can both see in your thoughts," it said. "She would never relinquish what we offer."

Margot shouted, "Ava! I know you can hear me. You have the power to stop the horror tearing this city apart!"

The Ava-thing dropped from the ceiling, approaching Margot and Sebastian with unsettling grace. Its eyes glowed malevolently, radiating an insidious intent; it flexed its grotesque limbs in anticipation.

Margot focused her thoughts on the amulet around her neck. Channeling her energy, she spoke an incantation, unleashing the power of the charm. Brilliant light enveloped the Ava-thing, trapping it within a ghostly cage.

But the victory was short-lived as the Ava-thing broke free from the containment spell, its form twisting with newfound fury. With a malicious grin, it lunged at Margot, looming over her, its claws poised for a lethal strike.

After a two-hour search in the dimly lit secret sanctum of Midnight Curiosities, Victor Blackwood discovered a crucial reference. Candlelight cast dancing shadows on the weathered tome of forgotten knowledge. Margot peered over his shoulder as they learned that the paintings of *Buluc-Chabtan Ucan* were made using the cursed Brush of Whispers. These artworks were said to unleash ancient eldritch beings that sowed discord, madness, and despair, feeding off the chaos they unleashed upon the world.

The painting, "Infernal Descent," a relic housed in Victor's shop, was the sole surviving piece made with the Brush of Whispers, its curse supposedly removed by an alchemist. This confirmed Margot's belief in the connection between Ava's haunting and the city's pandemonium.

Victor looked up curiously. "What led you to the Infernal Descent?"

Margot raised an eyebrow. "I remember seeing it in your shop. Its macabre style perfectly matched my client's. It couldn't be a coincidence."

Victor returned to the texts. He discovered that deciphering the answer from the Infernal Descent was necessary to seal the dimensional gateway.

Margot was already ahead of him, visualizing the painting in her mind. She knew what she had to do. When she explained it to Victor, he shuddered.

Margot reached out and shook his hand. "Thank you, Victor. You really came through."

"Think nothing of it," he said. "Not after all the business we've done."

Sebastian stretched on a velvet chaise lounge before leaping to the floor. He gazed at Victor and said, "I may have judged this cloistered bookworm too harshly. He's a veritable bibliophilic archaeologist."

Margot ignored the comment and turned to leave, followed by her feline familiar.

Victor cleared his throat. "Oh, Sebastian. . ."

Sebastian and Margot stopped cold.

"This cloistered bookworm has always been able to perceive you." The shopkeeper seemed rather satisfied with the looks on their faces as he returned to his books.

The Ava-Thing's ruined face hovered inches from Margot's, its mandibles wide open.

"Ava, listen to me!" Margot's voice pierced the suffocating darkness. "Take control, if only for a moment. Save your soul!"

The Ava-Thing twitched, jerked back an inch, wrestling for internal dominance. With an anguished cry, Ava managed to grasp a fragment of influence, forcing her transformed hands toward Margot.

It was clear she understood the sacrifice needed.

Momentarily freed from the invisible restraints, Margot drew her sword. Its gleaming blade reflected the last vestiges of Ava's humanity. With a swift, resolute strike, she amputated the monstrosity's hands, severing the eldritch connection. An explosion of alien energy engulfed the room, banishing the malevolence to its realm and restoring Ava to her true self.

In a final act of cosmic sorcery, Ava's once-prized artworks dissolved into the void, leaving the walls barren, a dark reminder of lost dreams and the cost of tampering with arcane forces.

Margot retrieved a healing salve brewed with witchcraft from an inside pocket. She would seal Ava's wounds until an ambulance arrived.

Sebastian raised his voice above the rumble of the turbocharged Mustang. "All of that work gone. . .hands gone. . .and Ava cast back to obscurity. That brush exacts a high price."

Margot grunted and shifted into fourth gear.

"Then again, I suppose that's one way to escape artistic criticism. Lose the hands."

"Too soon," Margo replied.

Sebastian huffed and settled more comfortably in the passenger seat. "What will you do with it? The brush, that is."

Margot raised an eyebrow. "Thinking of taking up painting? Might be tough with those paws."

"Too soon," the cat said, smirking, and closed his weary eyes. The engine's hum eventually lulled him to sleep.

A WHITER SHADE OF CHRISTMAS

MATT CONNOR HAD already lied to fourteen people since he'd arrived at the office and it was only 11:00 am. He didn't like lying, partly because he'd never been any good at it. But he'd told this particular lie so many times over the past five holiday seasons, he'd almost convinced himself of its veracity. Besides, there wasn't much risk of being caught. No one had any real reason to suspect him. After all, why would anyone continually lie about something as innocuous as Christmas plans?

Matt glanced around at the honeycomb of cubicles that spread across the entire 5th floor. There were only a few stragglers left, all of them pretending to work. It was ridiculous to expect anything else. It was common knowledge that no one worked on Christmas Eve unless they had already used up their vacation time earlier in the year—or like Matt—weren't in any particular hurry to get home.

Bill Girard, a lanky man with salt and pepper hair, stopped by Matt's cubicle en route to the kitchen. He had a particular way of holding his empty coffee cup, dangling it by its handle from his index finger. He swung it see-saw fashion continuously as he spoke.

"So. . .what's your excuse?"

"Hmm?" Matt didn't look up, pretending to concentrate on his work.

"You must have a million vacation days saved up by now. Why are you here?"

"Just trying to tie up loose ends before the long weekend," Matt said. It was his fifteenth lie for the day. At this rate, he might as well notch up another couple to break his record.

"Your family is local, right?"

Matt nodded.

Bill offered a bitter grimace. "Mine too. . .unfortunately."

"That bad?"

"Are you kidding? They should have their own reality show."

Matt laughed. Maybe for the first time that week.

"All right, amigo, "Bill said, "I'll leave you to it. But don't stay too late. The boss said we could split at noon today."

Matt raised an eyebrow. "He actually said that?"

"Either that or 'Stop stealing the office supplies', I can't remember which."

Matt smirked. "Get outta here. And have a nice Christmas."

"You too."

And then Bill was gone.

Matt sighed and tried very hard to focus on his monthly marketing report. But all he could think about was his plan for the next day.

On his way home, Matt bought a $136 bottle of Caymus Cabernet Sauvignon, a special treat that he allowed himself once a year on Christmas. It was a holdover from a tradition he began as a bachelor years ago. He would prepare a massive Christmas feast for close friends who were either stuck in town for the holidays or didn't have any family in Los Angeles to spend it with. It became known as the *Great Orphan Christmas* and at the height of its popularity, he was preparing dinner for as many as twenty people.

Later, his wife Emma insisted that they continue the tradition, which spoke volumes about her, he thought. For the first three years of their marriage, they worked together every Christmas to make it a special time for their many "orphaned" friends.

It was a beautiful thing. A perfect thing. But now it was no more.

Matt parked his Honda Accord on the street and ambled toward his apartment complex, briefcase in one hand and the bottle of wine in the other. Immediately, he spotted a familiar figure moving toward him along the sidewalk: a homeless man named Lucas, who had a smile as big and sincere as his heart. As usual, he was pushing his rusted shopping cart with the forever-squeaking wheels. Matt made a mental note to buy him some WD-40.

A WHITER SHADE OF CHRISTMAS

"Merry Merry," Lucas said, and his smile, like his presence, was genuine and kind. Lucas often said words twice for emphasis. It was one of his many endearing qualities.

"Merry Merry," Matt replied with a grin. In spite of Lucas's reduced circumstances, it was hard not to grin when he was around. Matt saved up all of his glass, aluminum, and plastic recyclables for Lucas, who picked them up regularly for his recycling run twice a week.

However, on this particular evening, Lucas' shopping cart wasn't filled with recyclables—it brimmed with canned food and other non-perishable items. And there was a recently hand-painted sign attached to the side of his shopping cart which read:

COLLECTING CHRISTMAS DINNER FOR MY FAMILY.

Matt was surprised, and it showed. He'd never imagined Lucas had a family to support. "I. . .didn't know you had family out here."

Lucas winked. "Well, we only get together once a year."

"I see," Matt said, still thrown by the idea Lucas needed to collect food for his family. "Are they. . .around here. . ." Matt's voice trailed off. He didn't want to risk offending the older man.

"Not far from here, over on Havelock Street, just west of the freeway."

Matt didn't know what to make of this. "Can I. . .offer you and your family something for tomorrow?"

Lucas gave a dismissive wave with a dirt-encrusted hand. "You do enough, my friend."

"Well—someone gave me this bottle of fine wine and I'll never drink it. Maybe someone in your family would like it?"

Lucas eyed the bottle and gave a short wolf whistle.

"I never heard of that brand, but I know that ain't no screw cap label."

Matt thrust the bottle into Lucas' hands. "Please, I insist."

"Well, I suppose. It wouldn't be right to turn down a Christmas gift."

Matt grinned and slapped Lucas on the shoulder. "Wish your family a Merry Christmas for me, will you?"

"Absolutely. Absolutely. You do the same, y'hear?"

Matt just smiled and walked toward his apartment.

He was almost at his front door when Lucas called out to him.

"Hey," Lucas said, shuffling to catch up. "You mind if I ask you somethin'?"

Matt turned back, "Sure."

"You got plans for tomorrow?"

Matt was a bit startled by that. Was Lucas that canny? Or was his loneliness that obvious?

He didn't want to lie to the man. Not Lucas, of all people. So, he told him the truth. . .or an aspect of it. "Yes, I'm visiting someone across town."

Lucas' eyes met his. "Well," he said. If you can make the time, we'd surely be honored if you'd come by for some dinner. I'll save some of this fine wine for ya."

Matt was touched. "That's very thoughtful of you. But I'll be gone until late tomorrow evening." That part wasn't true, and he felt his voice quiver as he said it.

"No problem, no problem," Lucas said. "Tell you what. . .we'll have a drink in your honor, how about that?"

Matt felt his heart sink at the realization that Lucas might think he'd turned down his offer because of his appearance or itinerant status. Nothing could have been further from the truth. Backpedaling, he said, "I tell you what, if I get home early enough, maybe I can stop by. Where do you live?"

⇶⟫⟪⇷

The next morning on the way to his appointment, Matt thought about Lucas' odd response to the question of where he lived. He'd remained typically vague about any details of his life, but apparently, he didn't have a permanent home. Meanwhile, his family lived in a house in a decent neighborhood not far from Matt's place. He had to admit that a part of him wanted to make an appearance simply to understand what it all meant.

As he stepped from his car and walked through the gates, Matt surveyed the cedar trees dotted about, the headstones stretching into the distance, and the grounds, which were as hard and cold as he had felt all week long. He cleaned a year's worth of bird excrement from Emma's black marble headstone with Windex and half a roll of paper towels. When he was finished, he glanced about nervously and lay along her grave for several minutes, breathing in the cool December air. Dark clouds marched in from the east and gradually blocked the sun.

He reached over to the portable mp3 player he'd brought along and selected the song he played every year: "Whiter Shade of Pale" by Procol Harem. On their honeymoon, he and Emma had slow danced to it on the patio of a cabin they had rented in Taos, New Mexico. Later, he replayed the song as they made love.

From that point, it had become "their song."

The first time Matt had visited Emma at the cemetery, he'd brought a framed picture of her and held it tightly in his hands as he played their song. For a moment, he'd even started to sway back and forth with the picture, a re-enactment of their slow dance together. The tears just wouldn't stop that Christmas day.

But now, five long years later, as the chorus of the song began, what normally made Matt feel connected to Emma left him cold. He turned it off halfway through. For a long while he stared out over the silent landscape of gravestones, dead hopes, and forgotten dreams. He knew he couldn't continue this ritual forever. The first time had been to honor the anniversary of her death. And the next couple of years it felt like the right thing to do. But now he dreaded Christmas like a terminal case of cancer.

He felt a terrible pang of guilt for feeling that way. But he also knew that Emma wouldn't have wanted him to experience such profound loneliness year after year. Since her death, he'd managed to gradually push the world away, despite countless attempts by his friends to keep him in contact with it. Emma's parents were from England, and maintaining a relationship with them after her funeral had been awkward and strained. He hadn't spoken to them in over three years. As for his own family, Matt was an only child. He'd never known his father and had lost his mother to leukemia when he was nineteen years old.

A pigeon soared overhead just then and landed on a small headstone several yards away. As Matt studied the slate gray bird, he thought it looked both sad and lonely perched amongst the dead.

He couldn't bear to stay a moment longer; he rose to his feet and brushed dust and grass from the legs of his pants. Gently, he pressed his lips against the laser-etched image of Emma set into her gravestone; the image was flat, and cold, and he could already see it was beginning to fade.

As he started back toward his car, he glanced over to where the lonely pigeon had landed.

But it was not to be seen.

Matt spent the rest of the day cooking as if his life depended on it. Every year it was the same: he prepared an elaborate Christmas dinner for one and ate leftovers for a week after. It gave him purpose on a day when the entire city seemed to shut down. And it was a welcome distraction from what felt like the longest day of the year.

The main dish, of course, was the stuffed turkey—emphasis on the stuffed. Over the years, he'd developed his special recipe for the stuffing, which consisted of day-old French bread, walnuts, currants, martini olives, and a handful of secret spices that he'd only shared with Emma. In years past, he'd taken pride in the fact that there was never a speck of stuffing left when it was time to wash the dishes.

Early in the afternoon, a strange idea began to form in Matt's mind. A possibility he never would have imagined twenty-four hours earlier. It both thrilled and terrified him—and he vacillated over it for several hours. When he'd finally completed his meal preparations, he stood in the center of his kitchen, and wiped sweat from his furrowed brow, taking stock of the steaming pots and pans. He'd made a huge bowl of mashed potatoes, a platter of corn on the cob, a pile of yams, thick homemade biscuits, and two pumpkin pies from scratch. It felt both pathetic and selfish to hoard such a glorious feast.

As the antique grandfather clock in the hall chimed five times, he made his decision.

Matt's chest tightened as he schlepped up the steps of the well-kept, but modest home on Havelock Street, to knock on the door of a family he'd never met, carrying bags filled with enough food to feed a small country.

What if they've already eaten? What if bringing all this food offends them? What if Lucas spoke out of turn and no one really wants me here? How ironic that I might be the charity case in this situation.

A WHITER SHADE OF CHRISTMAS

Not that he'd brought the food out of charity. Cooking for others was one of his greatest joys, and he loved its almost magical power to connect people.

He knocked three times on the door, anxiety growing with each thud of the metal doorknocker. When the door opened moments later, Matt's breath caught in his throat. A stunning natural beauty—mid-thirties, he guessed—stood before him with a lovely smile. She appeared to be of Hispanic descent, her delicate features framed in jet-black hair that dropped to her waist. "You must be Matt with the expensive taste," she said with an exotic accent he couldn't quite place.

Matt offered a self-conscious grin, "Oh. . .the wine. I hope you like Cabernet Sauvignon."

She smiled again, and dimples formed in her cheeks. "Lucas wouldn't let anybody open it until you got here. . .and that wasn't easy with *this* crowd,"

Matt chuckled. Any trepidation he had felt seemed to drain away in her presence. It was like standing near the warmth of a cozy fire on a chilly winter's night. "I'm Gabriela," she said while reaching for two bags near his feet. "Let me help you with those."

"I hope you don't mind that I brought some food along."

"Actually, you saved me. We had a bigger turnout than I expected this year."

The inside of the home was unassuming in its simplicity. Modern lines of brushed metal shelves and furnishings were tempered with thick blankets and a few pillows in warm, earthen tones and geometric patterns, patterns reflected in the upholstery of the couch and loveseat, and the area rug in the middle of the cream-carpeted living room.

As they stepped through the main living area and toward the dining room, Matt took note that there wasn't a thing out of place as far as he could tell. If Gabriela kept the house, she took a great deal of pride in her humble abode.

Matt could hear Lucas' booming laughter and a cacophony of voices talking at once. As they entered the dining room, he was surprised to see that it was filled to maximum capacity. There were several cheap folding tables shoved together, and around them sat a rough-looking group of men and women who looked like they had just come in off the street.

And, in fact. . .most of them had.

When Lucas had referred to his family, it had been a figure of speech. His "family" was a gathering of people who had either lived or were living on the streets, and all were veterans of various wars, including Vietnam, the Persian Gulf, and the invasions of Afghanistan and Iraq.

Matt found it difficult to tell some of their ages. Most looked older than their years, faces masked by the cruel scars of their hard lives. Lucas was wearing the same clothes as the day before, but it looked like he'd made a moderate attempt to clean himself up. His normally bushy hair was slicked back, and he'd managed a shave.

Matt sat between Lucas and an elderly African American man named Jamin, who had lost both his legs in Vietnam. He had the eyes of a man who had seen a lot and lamented over much of what he had observed. It was something that many of the group shared in common.

Matt learned that the home belonged to Gabriela and that she had lost her husband—U.S. Army Corporal Luis Cardona—three years previously in the invasion of Iraq. Luis was mentioned fondly during the evening, and several spoke of his great empathy for homeless veterans. At one point or another, he had helped everyone at the table through various volunteer programs, and it had been his idea originally to have them over for Christmas dinner. Gabriela had carried on the tradition since his death.

When he had first sat down at the table, taking in the haggard faces of the fifteen men and two women there, he had worried that he was in for a more depressing night than he would have had on his own. Matt was well-read and familiar with the travesty of homeless veterans in the United States: men and women who had dutifully served their country, only to be forgotten by it when they were of no more use to it. A few of the guests had obvious physical ailments, including one man—Kenneth—who suffered from the long-term effects of chemical toxin exposure. But not everyone's situation was as obvious. Matt remembered that a large percentage of homeless veterans suffered from post-traumatic stress disorder, causing everything from debilitating depression to substance abuse, aggressive behavior, and a spectrum of severe mental illnesses precipitated by the stress of war.

As the evening progressed, he discovered that not everyone at the table was homeless. A few had found steady work and improved their lives through the local volunteer programs Luis had been involved with. They returned to Gabriela's Christmas dinner to honor Luis' memory and to stay in touch with their "family".

Lucas, while a sociable man by nature, normally didn't talk about the details of his life, preferring to quote batting averages, won-lost records, and other sports statistics he gleaned from radio sports news. But on this particular occasion, he seemed more open to discussing his situation.

"The military dictates everything you do, man—and that's not me," he told Matt while digging into a pile of mashed potatoes. "These days I sleep on a nice mattress in my Chevy van, wake up when I want, eat three squares a day, and shower at the YMCA. My day job is collecting cans, and it's good for the community. When I'm not working, I'm at the library reading books or using their computers. It's not a fancy life, but it works for me."

Lucas was one of the lucky ones. Matt watched, listened, and spoke to the various people at the table and he realized that while he had lost the love of his life, many of them had lost everything. Some were still scraping by on the fringes of society by any means necessary.

If anyone was ever justified in being depressed, he decided, it was most of the people in the room.

However, Matt was surprised at how upbeat the mood was. Most of the topics of discussion were things you would expect at any normal gathering of friends: travel, news, sports, and a few very bad jokes. There was laughter, fellowship, and camaraderie.

Though his life was much different to that of the rest of the group, they welcomed him as if he was an old friend. Throughout dinner, there were raves about his food that pleased him to no end. But secretly, his favorite moment was when Gabriela had placed her delicate hand on his arm and asked him to share his recipes.

After the evening's traditional toasts to Luis and Gabriela, Lucas made quite a show of Matt's "pricey grape juice," and proposed another. "We've gathered tonight to have fun, fellowship, and be grateful. . .because thanks to Matt's bottle. . .we're not drinking from a screw cap label."

After the laughter subsided, he added. "But in all seriousness. I'd like to propose a toast to our guest, Matt Conner. A man I'm happy to call 'friend,' but am even happier to call 'family.'"

Matt flushed as everyone clapped. Lucas and several of the guests stayed after dinner to help clean up, but it was Matt who insisted on finishing the dishes, despite Gabriela's protests. Lucas quickly caught on that he was the third wheel and said his goodbyes. "See you next Tuesday," he said to Matt, referring to his usual recycling run. He hugged Matt and squeezed him so hard that he nearly took his breath away. "She likes you," he whispered, offering a knowing wink.

And then Lucas was gone.

Gabriela washed dishes while Matt dried. The room was quiet for the first time since Matt had arrived. There was a rhythm to their work as if their movements were synchronized. But after a few minutes, the silence started to become awkward. Matt sensed an attraction between them, but it was also a bit uncomfortable.

"Umm. . ." they both said simultaneously and then laughed nervously.

"You were about to say something?" Matt said.

"I was going to say that Lucas was right about you."

Matt raised an eyebrow.

Gabriela met his eyes. "You're a special person." She said it as if her conclusion had come from careful observation.

"I was about to say something similar. Opening your house to all of these people. . .it's a rare thing."

Gabriela finished rinsing a saucepan, "I can't take all the credit—it was my husband's idea. "

"He sounds like a great man. I'm sorry for your loss."

She offered a nod of acknowledgment.

"Where are you from originally?" Matt asked.

"Honduras. Do you know it?"

"I've never been, but I'm familiar with it."

"It's a beautiful country. But I grew up in one of the worst parts of it."

"Is your family here?"

She handed him the saucepan to dry. "No, my family is still scattered around Honduras. I visit now and again, but my life is here now—thanks to Luis."

"You both came from Honduras?"

"He was my neighbor growing up," she said. She stopped cleaning for a moment and stared pensively through the kitchen window, out toward the night sky. "We saw a lot of terrible things together. He was always protecting other kids in the neighborhood, including me. When we were teenagers, he started talking about coming to America and I used to tease him about it. But I also made him promise to bring me with him."

"I'm glad," Matt said.

The corners of Gabriela's lips curved upward as she started cleaning a rack of glasses. "What about you—any family?"

"It's. . .complicated," Matt said and immediately regretted it. He was so used to deflecting questions about his family with elusive answers that he did it automatically. He didn't want anyone's pity, and normally, the average person wouldn't bother to probe further than the first couple of questions.

"I see. . ." her voice trailed off as if contemplating his answer. After a few moments of cleaning, she turned to him. "I've always liked complicated stories"

Matt grinned. Her genuine interest disarmed him, and he was surprised to find that he wanted to tell her about his life. Though he'd only known her a few hours, it was the first time in years that he'd felt comfortable enough to talk about Emma, her death, and how difficult it had been to face the world without her. Perhaps it was because Gabriela could relate to losing a spouse.

So, he told her everything: how he'd met Emma during a time when he didn't know who he was, or where he was going. How she had seen something in him that he hadn't seen in himself. How she inspired him to finish college, get his business degree, and eventually work his way up to a senior position at a top marketing agency.

Gabriela didn't say a word. She listened intently as he told her how lost he'd been without Emma the first few years, and that lately he'd begun to resent the fact that he couldn't let her go.

When the room was quiet again, he could see the empathy in Gabriela's lovely brown eyes and knew that she understood. The hug they shared was spontaneous, a rare and special moment between widower and widow.

They completed the dishes, commiserating and laughing about some tragically bad dates they had both experienced through meeting people online.

It was past midnight when Matt started down the front steps of Gabriela's home, carrying two large bags filled with his empty food containers.

Gabriela watched him from the doorway as he started down the sidewalk. "See you next Christmas?" she called out.

He turned back with a grin. And this time, his words were neither guarded nor evasive. "Sooner, I think."

At that, Gabriela offered a smile that lit up her face like a Christmas tree.

Matt moved off down the street, swinging the two bags, and marveled at how light they were.

DON'T OPEN YOUR EYES

WILLOW HOUSE, as it was called by those who knew its grim history, seemed to shun the light, even in the brightest part of the day. The last house on the dead-end street of Willow Lane, it stood like a lone sentry; long forgotten, yet unwilling to abandon its post.

Inside its shadowy recesses, Jessica Lewis trudged up a flight of circular stairs to the second floor. Ahead of her, a young real estate agent tugged anxiously at his ill-fitting coat for what she guessed was the hundredth time.

The topic of missing persons had yet to come up, and the tour was nearly over.

The young man, whose name tag read 'Brandon', gestured for her to enter the master bedroom. Jessica empathized with his situation, of course. Espousing the virtues of mountain views and pegged hardwood flooring was one thing. Acknowledging that every previous owner of the house had gone missing on Halloween was quite another.

Brandon glanced around the room uneasily as he pulled back the curtains of the tall window to showcase the view. Jessica gave him another once-over and decided he couldn't be more than 23 years old. He looked like he was wearing his dad's suit in the hopes of appearing more professional.

She almost felt sorry for the kid; he would be easy to bulldoze.

The room smelled of emptiness, of things long forgotten, of people long gone. Jessica thought of the previous owners who had lived, laughed, made love, and perhaps died in this very room.

Brandon cleared his throat then, startling Jessica from her reverie. She was about to ask him about noise from nearby roads or neighbors, but he was already gesturing for her to follow him.

He spun on his heels and strode out of the room as if attempting to inject purposeful confidence into his movements.

Jessica had an arsenal of negotiation tactics she'd honed over the years, and the young agent had fallen for each of them.

As they stood in the home's reception hall, she talked him through a litany of repairs needed and overestimated costs on all of them. She noted that in his oversized suit, Brandon looked like a turtle withdrawing into its shell.

It seemed as if he wanted to escape the house, his eyes continually searching for. . .

What exactly? she thought. *The ghosts of the missing owners?*

Jessica stood in front of the door, blocking him. It was time to call out the elephant in the room.

She asked about the history of Willow House.

Brandon visibly reacted, glanced away, and then slowly returned her gaze.

In some states, real estate agents were required by law to disclose prior deaths in the house or anything significant that might devalue the property. This was not one of those states.

"Ms. Lewis. . ." Brandon said, clearing his throat. "Other than some of the minor repairs discussed, the seller hasn't mentioned any material defects, so I—"

Jessica cut him off with a dismissive wave. I already did my research, *Brandon.* "I know all about the previous owners. I just wanted to make sure you know that *I know.* So you'll understand the reasoning behind my final offer."

Jessica leaned in, self-assured, and gave him a low-ball number. Flustered, the young man mumbled something about discussing it with his client and rushed out the front door.

Jessica knew they would take it. The house was unsellable.

She would change that, of course.

That was her whole hustle.

Four months later, Jessica was living in the unsellable house on Willow Lane.

DON'T OPEN YOUR EYES

Ten years prior, she had figured out a great niche business: buying stigmatized properties at cut-rate prices and reselling them to unsuspecting buyers for a huge profit.

She jokingly coined the phrase 'Haunted Flips' to a few close friends to explain her business model. She'd move into allegedly haunted houses and renovate them to create forced equity. There were certainly financial advantages to buying as a homeowner rather than an investor, but it also gave her the ability to refurbish at her leisure. Plus, she rarely had to hire contractors because she'd learned to do many of the repairs herself over the years, further maximizing profit.

"Buy the worst house in the best neighborhood," her mentor had said early in her career, and while not always true, it had worked for her most of the time. "A great neighborhood is like a rising tide," he often repeated. "It will lift the price of all the homes around it."

Finding a buyer, though? That was the tricky part.

Jessica had spent years developing ways to lure in the trusting, the clueless, and the technology-challenged (if you couldn't use a search engine well, you couldn't investigate a house very well). She'd had particularly good luck transforming alleged haunted houses into vacation homes and selling them to international investors with poor English-speaking skills.

Now, it had been three days since moving into the house and Jessica hadn't seen anything creepier than a long-abandoned spider's web.

Typical, she thought, while inspecting one of the guest rooms. This was her thirteenth time living in a haunted house, and she'd yet to experience anything remotely supernatural. She found herself longing for an extraordinary encounter if only to break the monotony.

As she surveyed the room, it was clear it would be easy to renovate; it just needed fresh paint and a light refinish on the hardwood floor. She jotted down some notes and kneeled to take a closer look for any buckling in the hardwood. There was none, but what caught her eye were clumps of jet-black hair in several places, particularly against the baseboards.

She grimaced. The room hadn't had a thorough cleaning.

The hair was quite long; the kind usually reserved for the young. Was it the hair of one of the missing children?

She shook away the awful thought and went back to her notes, recalculating her budget. The bedrooms were going to cost even less than she'd planned.

Deal of the century, she thought.

Willow House was a two-story, brick Colonial-Revival style home with a gabled roof, a porch with a wooden bench swing, and an arched portico with classical columns. It had the simple symmetry and structure of the 1920s colonial style with a taste of Victorian-era architecture.

There had been some obvious renovation over the years, but the lack of regular upkeep was in stark contrast to the other well-maintained homes and manicured lawns along the affluent, willow tree-lined street.

The front yard was a jungle of overgrown shrubs, knee-deep grass, and weeds flourishing in the flowerbeds.

Inside were high ceilings and tall windows, along with intricate detailing and moldings. The second floor consisted of three bedrooms and a bathroom at the end of the hall, while the traditional first-floor layout included a reception hall, kitchen, living room, and dining room.

The sparse furnishings around the house were the most basic Jessica could procure, and what she referred to as her 'renovation starter kit'. There was no sense moving in more than the essentials since she would have to move everything out again in a relatively short amount of time.

Now, as she sat on her favorite 'traveling couch', calculating flooring costs, an aggressive *knock knock knock* shattered the silence of the living room.

Jessica grumbled under her breath and went to answer the front door.

Claire Vass had flawless skin, bright blue eyes, and came bearing cookies, gossip, and a barrage of questions. Jessica guessed she was in her 50s but easily looked ten years younger.

As the self-described '*cul-de-sac* welcoming committee', Claire never seemed to run out of words or the energy to use them. In the hour since her arrival, she'd managed to deluge Jessica with dirt on every single person living on the short street.

DON'T OPEN YOUR EYES

Mr. Kane, for example, was a pervert who watched animated porn on his big-screen TV with the shades open. Old Lady Livingstone was to be avoided at all costs unless one fancied a 3-hour rant about nothing. And perhaps, most important of all, she was advised to never step on Mr. Yarwood's lawn or touch any of his prized azaleas, or she would not live to regret it.

The conversation, which began at the front door, eventually moved to the wooden swing on the porch, which Jessica had wiped off as best she could with a rag.

"You're very attractive, you know," Claire said, examining her closely. Perhaps too closely. "Planning to get married? Kids?"

Jessica forced a smile; she had never accepted compliments well.

I'm not the settle-down type, lady, she wanted to say. *Plus, I'd rather gouge my eyes out than stay on this dead-end street any longer than I have to.*

Instead, she said, "You never know. But I love having my independence."

That was her personal shorthand—*I don't need to get married to be fulfilled, Claire. I love my career, love to travel, and I don't like wasting time on dating apps.*

Claire watched her for an uncomfortably long moment. Finally, she said, "Well. . .I think you're incredibly brave for buying this place. A single woman in a house with that kind of history? I admire you."

Jessica forced the umpteenth smile of the conversation. "No, I'd be brave if I *believed* in ghouls and ghosties, but I don't. It's just a fixer-upper to me."

Claire's phone buzzed and she quickly read a text.

"Oh, that's my husband, Bill, wanting lunch." She shook her head in mock disappointment. He can tell you how to fix a bad fuel injector, but still can't fix a ham sandwich without my help."

She reached over and gave Jessica an unwelcome hug. "I should get going. It was a delight getting to know you a bit better."

Then, as if remembering something, she reached for the plate of cookies she'd brought with her, now sitting on a nearby wicker chair. She folded back the aluminum foil to reveal homemade cookies in the shapes of pumpkins, black cats, and ghosts.

She handed them to Jessica as if they were spun from gold. "These are homemade, by the way; aren't they adorable?"

Jessica gave the woman her best *yes, they're adorable* grin and accepted the plate. "Really kind of you to bring these, thank you. Looks like you really like Halloween." *I mean, Christ, it's still September, lady.*

Claire smiled, but there was no warmth there. "Oh, we take Halloween *very* seriously around here."

She started down the porch steps and gave an odd little wave.

Jessica didn't wave back.

A week later, after a three-day trip to visit her mother, Jessica came home to something out of a blood-soaked nightmare. As she turned onto Willow Lane, she gasped. Everywhere she looked, there were relentless scenes of terror, torture, and mayhem.

Sure, she had seen neighborhoods that went all-out with Halloween decorations, but this looked like something borne out of Hell, a disturbing fusion of nihilism, rage, and carnage.

Realistic female mannequins were nailed to upside-down crosses and drenched in blood. Male and female figures were impaled on spikes and frozen in silent screams. A life-size child was half in and half out of a metal meat grinder, his lower half reduced to sludge in a red-stained bucket. Several lampshades appeared to be made from skin stitched together from human faces.

A family of four hung by their necks from the same thick branch, eyes bulging, duct tape stretched over their mouths. Some poor souls were sawed in half, while shredded limbs, glistening intestines, and gore-covered heads—some stuffed into large mason jars—were scattered about.

There were classic Halloween tropes as well, but not the silly decorations you picked up at the local drugstore. These skeletons, skulls, and animal skins looked alarmingly realistic. Several black cats seemed more likely to be authentic corpses stuffed by a second-rate taxidermist than the standard yard black cat. Carved pumpkins and turnips were illuminated from within by flickering candles, and oddly, plates of food were everywhere.

But what stood out most was the army of 7-foot-tall demons.

Normally, Halloween figures didn't bother Jessica, as they were not to be taken too seriously. Who hadn't seen a legion of store-bought mummies, vampires, or Frankenstein's monster at some point?

But there was something terribly *off* about these figures.

Positioned at strategic points amidst the contiguous yard displays, it was clear they were meant to be seen as the perpetrators of the blood-drenched chaos.

Jessica didn't recognize any of the grotesque things. She didn't know the names of such archaic European demons as a *Bánánach* or a *Fear Gorta*; she didn't know how to differentiate a bogeyman from an imp. But what she did know was that the realism in which they were portrayed was deeply unsettling.

They were murdering people. Shredding people. *Eating* people.

This isn't a celebration of Halloween, Jessica decided. *It's a celebration of depravity.*

As she finally reached the end of the cul-de-sac, she decided that the worst aspect of the whole sordid affair was the kids.

There were young children, smiling and posing amidst the offensive displays, parents laughing as they snapped photos with their phones.

What in the actual fuck–

Jessica slammed her car into the driveway and parked, hitting the brakes harder than she'd intended. She stormed towards her home, thought better of it, and turned again to see the *Grand Guignol* that had become Willow Lane.

Every house–except hers–had partaken in the madness.

She spotted Mr. Kane, facing her as he stood on his horror-themed lawn. He was an older man with wispy white hair and dressed smartly in black slacks and a maroon-colored shirt.

Wait–, she thought after a closer look. *That isn't maroon–it's soaked with blood.*

He was drinking what looked like an iced tea in one hand and offered her a friendly wave with the other as if it was just another day in suburban paradise.

Jessica didn't wave back.

It's October 1st, you twisted fuck. October 1st.

"We can't do anything about that, ma'am," the female police operator said on speakerphone. "Halloween decorations are protected by freedom of speech. We get calls about Willow Lane every year."

Jessica's breath caught in her throat, and she held back a torrent of expletives. "I find it very hard to believe the police are OK with these displays. They're disgusting, violent and horrifying. No child should be exposed to these kinds of things."

The operator didn't sound impressed. "Ma'am, it would have to be something way more graphic, something with profanity or nudity. If there was something written that was extremely offensive or a written threat, a real person's name, for example—then maybe we could do something."

"Great. You've been an incredible fucking help," Jessica said before hanging up.

She threw her phone onto the couch in exasperation. "It's October 1st for fuck's sake! I have a whole month of this shit?"

As Jessica paced the living room, she suddenly recalled a bizarre moment with Brandon, that little dweeb of a real estate agent, during her initial call about Willow House. One of the first questions he'd asked was if she celebrated Halloween.

She'd found that odd, of course, and after an awkward silence, told him it wasn't something she cared about either way. When she asked him why he wanted to know, he'd mentioned something about the neighborhood taking the celebration seriously. Jessica hadn't understood the context at the time and had quickly changed the subject.

She plopped onto the couch and rubbed her face, exasperated at the situation, which was as ludicrous as it was annoying. She thought about moving into a hotel for a few weeks or maybe staying with her mother up north until November.

But that meant that she'd lose a full month of renovation and that would throw her whole two-year schedule off. She was already looking into another "haunted" place near the coast that she wanted to buy as her next project. It had a large backyard, a tremendous view overlooking the coast, and frankly, was a bloody steal.

Jessica sighed. *No, they're not ruining my plans. I'll just keep my head down and stay busy renovating through most of October.*

However, that didn't mean she had to embrace her neighbors' Halloween madness.

Was madness even the right word?

Or was it a kind of. . .mass hypnosis?

She'd only had brief interactions with several of them. Mr. Yarwood talked endlessly about his azaleas, Mr. Kane tried—and failed, epically to flirt with her, and there had been one tortuously long conversation with Old Lady Livingstone that, as Claire put it, was about nothing.

They were annoying at most.

And yet, while Jessica didn't believe in the supernatural, she understood humanity's capacity for evil. The fact that all previous owners had gone missing on or around Halloween was not lost on her.

While she bristled at the idea of anyone thinking her superstitious, she was also no one's fool. Sometimes discretion was the better part of valor. It was at that point she decided she wasn't going to stick around for Halloween after all. From experience, she knew there was a lot she could accomplish in the next three weeks if she stayed focused.

Then, perhaps a few nights before October 31st, she'd slip out under the cover of night. Her mom would be thrilled at a surprise visit, and she could safely ride out Halloween far from the demented Willow Lane clan.

After today, she decided she would no longer interact with them. Lately, she'd gotten too loose with her personal code: never get close to neighbors during renovations. She'd learned the hard way that there were too many questions, and some people didn't take well to her mercenary view on house flipping.

She was there to turn a quick profit, not join a community.

With that decision firmly in place, she grabbed her tool belt with a look of grim determination and headed upstairs to get some renovation done. She hoped it would take her mind off the sick and twisted displays on Willow Lane.

Jessica evaded all communications with her neighbors over the next two weeks. Claire Vass dropped by unannounced *twice* and Jessica hadn't answered the door either time. She also didn't eat the Halloween-themed cookies Claire kept leaving on the porch.

She stopped returning friendly waves from nearby residents as she drove past the hellscape that was their lawns. She had food delivered often to reduce her trips to the grocery store; anything to avoid looking at those repulsive front yard displays or interactions with her neighbors.

However, the constant reminders of Halloween lurking in the background had piqued her interest in the subject. And after a few late-night web searches, she learned more about its history than she'd ever cared to.

Jessica was Welsh from her father's side, and she'd heard a little about Halloween's medieval origins in Europe when she was a child, but that was the extent of her knowledge.

Digging deeper, she learned that Halloween was a descendant of *Samhain*, a 2,000-year-old pagan religious festival celebrated by the Celts, halfway between the fall equinox and the winter solstice. Several sources claimed that ancient Celts believed the veil between the living and the spirit realm grew thinnest at this time, and all manner of supernatural beings could pass through as they pleased for one hallowed night.

Spirits, demons, and other beings from the Otherworld would cross over to cause mischief. So, the Celts placed offerings outside to satisfy them, in the hopes they wouldn't harm their livestock or storage of food.

In addition, they would light bonfires, carve frightening faces into root vegetables, and wear eerie masks and costumes made from animal skins, all in the name of warding off real demons and ghosts.

Conversely, she also read articles from historians and renowned Halloween authorities who dismissed all these ideas as erroneous, exaggerated, or frank bullshit. Some experts claimed that supernatural elements of Samhain's history were simply hyperbolized over generations to add mystique to Halloween's origins and sell more Halloween entertainment and merchandise.

Jessica much preferred that kind of logic, and yet as her web search deepened; she discovered illustrations depicting all manner of creatures from Celtic demonology. She was stunned that a few were strikingly like the demons displayed on Willow Lane. She recalled that many of the decorations looked archaic; right down to the candle-lit turnips.

She again thought of the experts' opinions and laughed out loud at the thought of upwardly mobile suburbanites warding off demons. Yet the idea lingered long after she'd shut down her computer. Had Willow House's haunted reputation caused a sort of mass paranoia on this street? Sure, maybe the supernatural aspect was bullshit, but was it possible her neighbors were simply delusional? Was it possible they were genuinely trying to drive away spirits and demons, as in some accounts of ancient *Samhain* tradition?

Jessica found it difficult to sleep, gazing up at the coffered ceiling for hours, contemplating the mysteries of the house.

When she'd discovered it earlier that year, all that mattered at the time was that it was a stigmatized property and had sat on the market for nearly twenty-five years, unheard of in such an otherwise great neighborhood.

The potential for profit is what excited her, not digging for information on missing people who were presumed dead.

As a real estate agent, she had plenty of tools at her disposal to investigate the history of a property, but she had never been one to seek out juicy details on grisly news items. She didn't watch true crime stories or slow down to stare at car crashes, and she certainly didn't delight in the tragedies or sufferings of others.

All she cared about was the unsavory reputation of the house and how much it devalued the property. The individual stories and details of its former owners were for ghost hunters, armchair sleuths, and lovers of the macabre.

However, even as a nonbeliever, Jessica had to admit there were some strange coincidences at Willow House. Perhaps most significant was that it remained unoccupied in twenty-five-year cycles, like clockwork. For another, no one had lived in the house longer than a year before they went missing. And most mystifying of all, the disappearances always occurred on or near Halloween. She noted that a couple of exact dates remained unconfirmed because two previous owners hadn't been listed as missing right away.

Definitely fucking creepy, she thought.

Now wide awake, Jessica found herself drawn to her laptop again. After booting it up, she began searching for news stories on the previous occupants of Willow House, of which there were plenty. All the disappearances remained unsolved. For this reason, most of the stories repeated the same information, offering nothing more than rumors and conjecture.

The most recent missing owners, Drew and Grace Campbell, an entrepreneur and travel nurse respectively, had been responsible for much of the modern renovations to Willow House. Constant world travelers, they were last seen on October 31st, 1997, the same day they returned after a three-month trip across Europe.

There had been no signs of a robbery or a struggle. All of their belongings were intact. It was as if they had simply vanished from the face of the earth. If they had left willingly, which was doubtful, they had taken nothing with them, including their cars.

The owners prior to that, back in 1972, were Stephen and Annie Valentine, and their children Christine and Jane. According to one story in a local paper, the Valentines were a conservative Christian family that didn't celebrate Halloween.

A diligent journalist had uncovered quite a bit of drama around the Valentines' offense at the neighborhood's elaborate Halloween decorations, which they said, quote, "celebrated demons and Satanism." Official complaints with the police had been filed and threats were exchanged.

The same article revealed that several neighbors had been questioned regarding the disappearance of the Valentine family in the days following Halloween. And while the term 'Persons of interest' was not yet in fashion, it was implied in the news story.

No arrests were ever made.

Jessica shook her head at the implications. Apparently, Willow Lane's overblown Halloween celebration went back to the 1970s. And it seemed she wasn't the only neighbor to take offense.

Now, fully down the internet rabbit hole, she learned that the owners before that moved into Willow House in 1947, the year the Cold War began between the U.S., the Soviet Union, and their allies. Floyd and Becca Probert, a dentist and a school administrator respectively, mysteriously vanished. No signs of a struggle, nothing was stolen, and their car was left behind.

They had been seen the night of October 31st, taking in a movie at the local theater. That was the last time they were heard from again.

Hours later, when Jessica had gone far back enough to research Finlay Henderson, the original owner of Willow House in 1922, information was scarce.

The few details available were that Finlay was a Scottish immigrant who had done well for himself in the newspaper business. Some articles praised the fact that a Scottish immigrant from such humble beginnings had accomplished so much in his ten years in America. Others called out the peculiarity of a single man buying a two-story, three-bedroom home for himself in 1922.

He was last seen on October 31st.

DON'T OPEN YOUR EYES

There was one interesting detail about Henderson, which stood out amongst all the others. According to several sources, police had discovered "strange, inexplicable symbols carved into the walls of the master bedroom," with one witness describing them as "magic sigils of some kind, possibly of European origin."

No one had been able to decipher their meanings.

Of course, this single detail was tremendous fodder for countless internet sleuths and ghost-hunting fanboys. Some posited that Henderson had carved the sigils into the walls to summon ancient demons for wealth and power. While others believed he had tried and failed to carve sigils to protect himself from something *inside* the house.

The fact everyone had disappeared on Halloween led some to speculate that the house served as a portal when the veil between the living and the spirit world was at its thinnest, as ancient Celts believed during *Samhain.*

It was at that point Jessica emitted a scornful laugh.

Stick to the Halloween experts, Jess, she thought, snapping her laptop closed for the night. *Forget the supernatural. This house ain't no fucking portal.*

As she reached across the bed to turn out the light, she glanced at the walls where Finlay Henderson had once carved the mysterious sigils. They were long gone now; the walls had either been replaced entirely or the carvings had been concealed with cladding and layers of wallpaper a hundred years old.

Jessica sighed heavily, turned out the light, and eventually fell into a fitful sleep.

She dreamt of unspeakable horrors lurking inside the walls.

October 31st was in four days and Jessica was so sick of the glorification of Halloween that she swore she'd never celebrate it again, even on the relatively mundane level she had in the past. For a while, she'd considered putting up the cheesiest, most absurd decorations she could find, just to ridicule her neighbors. But then she thought, *no, it's better to ignore the celebration entirely. That will let them know what I think of it.*

In the late afternoon, she realized a quick trip to the hardware store was needed to finish some minor touchups to the master bedroom. She'd already packed her suitcase and hidden it under blankets in the backseat of her car, eager to skip town after dark. As usual, she hoped to avoid any neighbors who tried to catch her eye.

Five minutes later, seven of them did.

They stood in the middle of the road having a heated discussion, and as a result, were blocking her car. She recognized some of them: Mr. Kane, Old Lady Livingstone, Mr. Yarwood, and right in the middle was Claire Vass talking up a storm, waving her arms excitedly.

They seemed to purposely ignore Jessica. Finally, she gave a light *honk* to get their attention.

In unison, everyone spun toward her, glaring at her intensely. Jessica felt a surge of fear rise in her chest.

Claire gestured to the group as if she were calming down a mob, said something that made them chuckle, and then sauntered up to Jessica's driver-side window with a smile from ear to ear.

"Well, hey stranger!" Claire gushed. "Y'know, I've stopped by twice to catch up with you. You must be a busy bee, hon. Buzz buzz."

Jessica gritted her teeth and forced a smile. "Yes, a busy bee, indeed. In fact, I need to get to the hardware store before they close. So, if you wouldn't mind. . .?"

She gestured to the glowering group standing in the middle of the road.

Claire leaned in, causing Jessica to lean back. "Y'know, hon, some of these folks are starting to think maybe you don't like our Halloween decorations. Tell me that's not true."

Jessica used every last ounce of self-restraint. "Look, if this is about me not decorating my home—"

Claire laughed. "No, no. . .you don't need to decorate *Willow House*. That's the scariest one on the block!" And then she laughed even harder.

Jessica steeled herself. "Claire. . .the hardware store closes in less than an hour."

"Oh right, sure. . ." Claire said and withdrew from the window. But then she leaned right back in, glancing around the interior of the car. "But you're planning to celebrate with us on Halloween, right? We're counting on everyone this year for the biggest turnout yet."

"Oh, definitely. . ." Jessica lied, offering the last smile she had left. *As in definitely getting the fuck out of Dodge tonight.*

DON'T OPEN YOUR EYES

"Wonderful," Claire said, clapping her hands lightly. Then she turned to the group in the road and shooed them away like a farmer scattering chickens.

Jessica drove past them, then looked back in her rear-view mirror as she reached the end of the street.

All seven neighbors stood silent and motionless, watching her drive away.

Jessica sighed with relief when she returned home, as there were no neighbors in sight. There were, however, a few random spectators taking photos with their kids amidst the Halloween grotesquerie.

Jessica stopped to let an obese family of three cross the street in front of her. As she sat in her idling car, she did her best to avert her eyes from the depraved street decor.

A name on a nearby mailbox caught her eye.

Scurlock. Where do I know that. . .?

She glanced at the nearest mailbox on the other side of the street, which read *Livingstone*. The next one after that read *Tallon*.

Jessica had a crazy thought, and when the pedestrians had cleared, she raced the rest of the way home. She wanted to get to her computer quickly and confirm those names.

Once she was inside and settled, Jessica crouched on the living room floor with her laptop, a half-eaten chocolate bar, and a nice *Pinot Noir*. She ordered a pizza with extra cheese and looked up articles she'd bookmarked from previous web searches.

It didn't take long to find what she was looking for.

In one of the more comprehensive articles about Willow House, she spotted the names Scurlock, Livingstone, and Tallon. The names on the mailboxes were the same as the neighbors mentioned in connection with the disappearance of the Valentine family back in '72.

They had been questioned extensively, but none were ever arrested.

Was it possible her neighbors were descendants of those families mentioned?

What about Old Lady Livingstone? If she'd been born and raised here, she was old enough to have been alive for all the previous owner disappearances except for Finlay Henderson back in 1922.

And what about the names themselves? Jessica was annoyed with herself that she hadn't noticed it before. She quickly did a web search to verify what she suspected.

She raised her glass to herself in a mock toast. "Fucking Sherlock Holmes over here, thank you. . ."

Scurlock, Livingstone, Tallon, and all the previous Willow House owners had either Irish, Scottish, or Welsh surnames.

She finished off the wine in her glass and thought about the neighbors she knew. Mr. Kane, the pervert, had an Irish last name. Old Lady Livingstone had a Scottish last name, while Mr. Yarwood, protector of the neighborhood azaleas, was Welsh. Nosy neighbor Claire Vass had a Scottish surname, and of course, Jessica's last name was Welsh.

That can't be a coincidence. And if it wasn't, what did it mean?

Then came a chilling thought. The Celts were an ancient group of people who lived more than 2,000 years ago in what is now Ireland, Wales, Scotland, and much of Europe.

Those same Celts who celebrated *Samhain*.

Jessica poured her third glass of wine. *Are you really following this line of thought, Jessica? Seriously.*

Suddenly, a loud *bang bang bang* at the front door. Jessica nearly spilled her wine.

She got up with a grunt and said, "That better not be fucking Claire."

It wasn't. She had forgotten she'd ordered pizza.

A teenage pizza delivery boy with blue-dyed hair and hands that shook stood in the cool night air. He was clearly nervous, his eyes darting to avoid Jessica's gaze.

"Sorry, I have to go grab my wallet," she said. "You want to come in out of the cold?"

"No, ma'am—I'm okay right here."

Jessica couldn't blame the kid. The house's reputation obviously preceded it, even with the local pizza joint. She gave him a nice fat tip for his bravery and quickly settled back into her investigation. The more she read, the more she was convinced she was making the right decision to leave town that night.

She would drive up north as a lovely surprise to her mother and stay for a full week or more. Her mother would be delighted.

DON'T OPEN YOUR EYES

Most importantly, she would miss several days before and after Halloween.

Jessica still didn't believe in curses, ghosts, or the supernatural, but when it came to being the owner of Willow House, the law of averages was undeniable. There was a big difference between superstitious and cautious.

But her escape plan was not to be.

An hour later, she barely made it to the toilet as a torrent of foul-smelling vomit erupted from her. The retching seemed endless, as if every ounce of fluid inside her was desperate to be purged from her body. She'd experienced food poisoning before, but this was far worse than any she'd known.

Her vision began to blur as darkness closed in around her.

Weak at the knees and quickly losing her equilibrium, her first thought was to call her mother. She rushed toward the master bedroom to grab her phone, but her legs gave halfway.

The last thing she remembered was the coppery taste of blood in her mouth.

Spinning blackness. Muted voices. Waves of nausea.

Jessica floated in and out of consciousness on an ocean of pain. She felt her limp body being lifted by several hands at one point. Later, she recognized the comfort of a bed, followed by more rolling darkness.

Daytime came and went. . .twice, three times, four. . .as if spirited away.

She dreamt of sigils, demons, and pumpkins filled with blood.

For a moment, she floated back up to the surface of consciousness, drawn to a familiar voice.

Was that Claire?

Jessica's eyes fluttered open, but her eyelids wouldn't cooperate. She caught a glimpse of several dark figures standing around the bed, watching her.

Claire's voice: "You gave her too much, you idiot."

A young male voice: "I'm sorry. . ."

"You could've killed her."

Jessica struggled to stay conscious, but the unrelenting blackness crashed down and dragged her back into its depths.

It was nighttime again when Jessica became fully conscious; memories stirred in her like dead leaves.

She suspected four full days had passed, which made it Halloween night.

But that was the least of her troubles.

Someone had first drugged and then shackled her to the bed in the master bedroom. Archaic-looking iron clasps held her wrists and ankles, shackling her arms and legs taut. She spent the first hour trying every conceivable angle to yank herself free, but this only resulted in torn and bleeding skin. The next hour was spent screaming for help.

No one came.

She remembered hearing Claire's familiar, grating voice. *You gave her too much, you idiot. You could've killed her.*

Who had she been talking to?

The pizza delivery boy. He drugged me.

It was at that moment Jessica confirmed there had never been anything supernatural about the house. The only thing to fear on Willow Lane were the neighbors.

How many generations did this madness go back? All the way to 1922? And to what end?

She started thinking about the disappearances of the other previous owners. Little details started to snap together like pieces of a mental puzzle.

She remembered the Valentines hadn't decorated for Halloween because of their religious beliefs. The Proberts were last seen taking in a movie on the night of October 31st, so perhaps they didn't celebrate either.

The Campbells had come back from a three-month trip to Europe, returning on Halloween day. It seemed unlikely they had decorated three months before they'd left. It wasn't hard to imagine they couldn't rush out to get decorations on the same day they returned when stores were already wiped out of decorations.

There weren't many details about Henderson in 1922, but Halloween didn't pick up steam until the 1930s in America, so it was likely he hadn't decorated either.

While every owner had an Irish, Scottish, or Welsh surname,

which was strange but not improbable, perhaps the most important common denominator was that none of them celebrated Halloween.

Were the denizens of Willow Lane that fucking insane? Had they killed the previous owners for not honoring the traditions of their ancestors?

But then Jessica had a far more disturbing thought. There was another possible connection with all the owners, including her. In the ancient celebration of *Samhain*, there were animal skin costumes, frightening faces carved into candle-lit root vegetables, demon and spirit masks, and more.

Together, they all had one singular purpose: protection.

So, what happened to those who didn't protect themselves? Was that an open invitation to entities from the Otherworld? Was there *something* on Willow Lane they needed protection from?

That was when Jessica noticed the sigils.

All along the walls and ceiling, they began to appear. Subtle outlines at first, as if drawn on tracing paper.

She tried to sit up to get a better look but to no avail. *No, that's fucking impossible. . .*

Moments later, they were deep red, like a branding iron, as if being heated in a forge.

Jessica shook her head and blinked her eyes. *I'm hallucinating. I must be. It's. . .an after-effect of the drug.*

A *thud* from somewhere in the house.

Jessica's head spun toward the bedroom door. From her vantage point, she had a good view of the hallway and the top of the circular staircase.

A *dark figure* was slowly crawling up the stairs. She heard a *creak.*

It didn't appear human.

Her eyes snapped shut as a subconscious reflex. She pretended to sleep; a child-like reaction to a situation in which she was trapped and vulnerable.

Just be still, she thought. *Please, God. . .*

Another *creak.*

Then. . .she felt a presence in the room.

Something was watching her.

All her senses seemed heightened. *What is that smell?* It reminded her of the musky, feral scent of her mother's cat.

A moment later, there was movement, if only slight.

It seemed to move along the wall. . .then the ceiling.

What is it? Her mind screamed, her heart hammering so hard she was sure it was audible to the thing in her room.

Thump!

It sounded as if it had dropped from the ceiling back down to the floor at the edge of her bed. A scream rose in Jessica's throat as if she were being roasted alive, but she held it back.

A moment later, she felt the mattress of her bed sink; the box springs groaned under the weight as something crawled in bed with her.

Jessica's shallow breathing became even more rapid, and tears streamed down her face. She'd managed to keep her eyes closed, but there was no disguising her fear now. The *thing* positioned itself so that she could feel its breath, which smelled like rotted meat, hot on her face.

Long, coarse hair brushed her cheek as it lowered its face toward hers, perhaps an inch away from her nose.

God. . .help me, please! Her mind shrieked.

A familiar sound then. At first, it seemed to be smacking its lips. But that wasn't quite right. In her imagination, she could see its wide lips stretching across a set of massive, glistening teeth.

The sound of a hideous smile.

Time moved as if it were a predator on a silent stalk; several terror-filled minutes passed but neither Jessica nor the thing gave an inch.

The experts had been the ones full of shit, after all.

Rain began to tap the window like an unwelcome guest, and Jessica heard it thrum and clatter on some broken roof tiles.

As long as I keep my eyes closed—I'm safe, she thought, as if trying to convince herself.

Somehow you know that too, don't you?

So, I'll just lie here.

And I'll never open my eyes.

Never.

Never. . ..

Outside the house, a slanted sheet of rain swept like a scythe across the backyard, where everyone who lived on Willow Lane gathered to stare up at her window.

Each was cloaked in animal skins, dressed as various demons from the Otherworld.

DON'T OPEN YOUR EYES

Claire Vass stood front and center beside her husband Bill. She had been fortunate to spot Jessica's suitcase peeking out from underneath a blanket in her backseat. She gave a silent prayer of gratitude.

As they continued to congregate, Mr. Kane held the arm of Old Lady Livingstone to make sure she didn't slip in the rain. Behind them were Mr. Yarwood and his blue-haired son, Dylan, who had paid off a pizza delivery person and laced Jessica's food.

Claire spoke in an ancient Celtic language as she traced sigils in the air with one finger.

The others began to do the same in a synchronized fashion for several minutes until the ritual was complete.

Brandon, the real estate agent, looked satisfied as he stepped up toward his father. He whispered, "Thought she was *so* smart. Thought she'd hustled us."

Mr. Kane offered a pleased smile, knowing everyone could expect twenty-five more years of prosperity. Proudly, he placed his hand on the young man's shoulder. "You did well, son. She was a perfect sacrifice."

As the rain grew in intensity, the denizens of Willow Lane continued to stare up at Jessica's window, waiting.

THE SHUDDERING BREATH BEFORE OBLIVION

BRIMPOOL HAD A way of swallowing souls, spitting out only whispers and ghosts.

Alex Riven, an investigative journalist more used to chasing shadows than sunlight, currently found himself stuck with the crummy end of the stick—getting to the bottom of a mystery in this washed-up seaside town. He was bellied up to the bar in the Salty Dragon, a place that had all the charm of a dead jellyfish washed up on shore. His notes, which were about as useful as a glass hammer, lay scattered in front of him as he sipped a watered-down drink.

His afternoon trip to the local cop shop had been a complete washout. Flashing his Eclipse Online press pass gained him nothing but disdain. The chief, a guy with a face like an overcooked ham, had given him the brush-off, telling him there weren't any ghost stories in Brimpool—just real problems, for real people. It was clear they thought he was just another media vulture sniffing around for a headline that would sell.

Peeved but not yet beaten, Alex had stormed out of the station, his hands as empty as when he'd walked in—full of questions and that itchy feeling at the back of his neck that told him something was off in Brimpool.

The growing number of disappearances wasn't just some blip to fill space on Eclipse Online's website. No, this smelled like something sinister lurking beneath the town's calm surface, something the police were either unable or unwilling to confront. Alex's mind was a battleground of doubt and resolve. How had it come to this? The days when his byline meant something were a distant memory. Now, he found himself beached in the dim glow

THE SHUDDERING BREATH BEFORE OBLIVION

of the Salty Dragon, in a world where the deep dive of journalism had been traded for the shallow splash of sensationalism.

A disastrous bygone headline now haunted Alex's career, the specter of a story too wild to be true—yet at the time, he'd bought it, staked his reputation on sources that vanished like smoke. That story was to be his crowning glory. But instead, it hung around his neck like a millstone of shame. Now, at Eclipse Online, he was reduced to hunting down leads on the fringe, tales whispered in the dark corners of the world, each one, he hoped, a chance to scrub away the stain on his name.

The truth, though—that unattainable, slippery truth—had become as scarce as wings on a wombat in the news game. The meaty stories, the ones you chewed on and couldn't let go, seemed to have all but disappeared, leaving behind a junk food diet of fluff pieces and listicles. Eclipse might have been the boondocks of the journalistic world, but for Alex, it was a place to dig in, a last stand where maybe, just maybe, he could find a story solid enough to plant his feet on and start the climb back up.

He took another sip of his cocktail, weak as a promise on April Fool's Day, and listened to the ice cubes clatter against the glass like hollow bones. That sound was like the empty spaces in Brimpool where people used to be. And somewhere in that hollow ringing was also the echo of the journalist he used to be, the one who used to chase the truth until it bled ink onto the front page.

He could feel that old itch as tales of the missing whispered to him. Mara Jennings, the dedicated teacher, had vanished into the misty morning without a trace, her car abandoned near the sea cliffs. Then there were the Andersons, a whole family gone, leaving behind a dinner table set for a meal that was never finished. And old Henry Marsh, who spoke of shadows warping reality, before he too slipped away. These missing people's stories, and a growing list of others, were becoming his—the chapters he'd write, or maybe the epitaph of his career.

The bartender appeared as if summoned by the final clink of ice against the glass. The brass nameplate declared her "Lucy", but it was her natural, effortless beauty that caught Alex's eye, her hair pulled back, not just for practicality, but as if to frame the honest story of her face. It spoke of a life lived fully. Time had softly molded her, not diminishing her allure, but rather enriching it with a mature grace.

"Another?" Her voice danced over the bar's hum, her hand pausing in its routine swipe across the counter. The dim bar light played across her features, highlighting her strong bone structure and the confident tilt of her head.

"Why not?" he said with a grin. "They can't get any worse."

Lucy's eyebrows arched, with her smile a silent challenge. "Does that mean you're an optimist. . .or a masochist?"

"Optimism died early in my journalism career," he said with a wry grin. "Occupational hazard."

"A masochist, then," she said.

He gave her a flirtatious look. "Depends on who is doing the torturing."

Their banter wove a warm tapestry in the cold bar. When Lucy served up the next drink, it was stronger—a quiet salute to their budding rapport.

Lucy, with the Salty Dragon's legacy running through her veins like saltwater, shared tales of her father, a man as rugged and storied as Brimpool itself. Her childhood was a tale of ocean lore, of lives embraced by the sea and those mysteriously swept away, leaving only whispers behind. It was a heritage rich with the echoes of the past, cradled in her care with a solemn pride.

However, as she discovered Alex's purpose in Brimpool, her wariness became palpable. The subject of the disappearances struck a sensitive chord. Yet Alex, seasoned in the art of conversation, navigated through her reservations with genuine interest and lighthearted humor, gradually easing the tension between them.

She opened up a bit, hinting at her personal theories without fully committing to them. "People talk," she said, her voice lowering. "They whisper about things they can't explain. But genuine insights? Well, that's as rare as a pearl in a pigsty."

As the night wore on and other bar conversations were overheard, Alex glimpsed the raw edge of fear the disappearances had carved into the town's heart. This was a thread, however slender, weaving through the fabric of Brimpool's mysteries, more tangible than anything he'd grasped yet. The night deepened, the bar's buzz dimmed, yet he found himself anchored by the siren call of Lucy's half-revealed secrets.

In a quiet moment, Lucy finally shared a piece of her own story. "Even my Grandpa Roman," she murmured, her voice a bridge to a past both personal and shrouded, "was taken. Here one day, gone the next."

The revelation of her grandfather, a direct tie to the enigma of the vanishings, honed Alex's interest to a fine point. There was an actual lead, a name that breathed life into the rumors, a personal connection to the heart of Brimpool's darkness.

As Lucy continued, Alex's thoughts raced. He recognized the edge he'd stumbled upon with Lucy, feeling a twinge of guilt at the thought. The evening's unexpected turn, blending flirtation with journalistic probing, had opened a path he hadn't anticipated.

His career had honed this balancing act: extracting pivotal information while preserving his moral compass. The real test lay ahead—in Brimpool's shadowed corners and whispered secrets. He sensed a story that could redefine his career.

As the evening wound down and the last of the patrons trickled out of the Salty Dragon Lounge, Lucy began the routine task of closing up. The clink of glasses and the shuffle of chairs filled the space, a comfortable backdrop to the charged silence that had settled between her and Alex.

He helped where he could, stacking chairs and wiping down tables, the shared tasks creating an easy camaraderie. Finally, with the bar looking more like a ghost town than a local haunt, Lucy turned to Alex, a playful yet tentative smile on her lips. "You know, I've got a decent bottle of whiskey at home. Consider it an apology for the watered-down drinks."

Her invitation hung in the air, a bridge between professional curiosity and personal interest, laden with unspoken possibilities.

"Lead the way," he said, accepting the invitation with a mix of anticipation and resolve. As they left the bar together, the cool night air of Brimpool felt less oppressive, charged with the promise of uncovering secrets hidden in the dark.

⇒⟫⟪⟪

Morning unfurled its light through the curtains, spilling warmth over the disarray of sheets that bore witness to the night's activities. Alex and Lucy's conversation meandered, weaving through soft confessions to the raw truths that only such closeness can coax into the open.

Lucy's laughter, light yet tinged with an elusive depth, punctuated the silence. "I'm not always this easy, y'know," she announced, her fingers absentmindedly tracing patterns on the fabric between them, hinting at intimacy without direct touch. "But there's something about men who seem to guard their warmth. Like you." Her gaze, intense and probing, pierced right through him.

"Do I guard my warmth?" Alex's voice revealed a hint of vulnerability.

"You are. . . shielded," Lucy said with a gentle smile. "Your eyes are wary, but observant. That's what caught my attention. I get the impression you're always searching. . . always digging."

Alex felt both understood and misinterpreted. His life, a mosaic of stories told and released, had conditioned him to view the world with detachment.

"There is some truth in that," he found himself saying, a raw honesty in his voice. "It's less about digging and more about understanding. I spend a lot of time sifting through life's chaos, searching for some semblance of the truth, I guess." The admission hung in the quiet between them, met by Lucy's understanding nod. Her openness presented an opportunity to explore Brimpool's mysteries from a new angle—through the eyes of someone intimately acquainted with loss. "You suggested that everyone here has their theory," he ventured, carefully. "That must be hard, living in a town with endless speculation."

Lucy paused before speaking. "It changes you," she said, her voice echoing the town's shifted atmosphere. "People try to dismiss it as coincidence, but the doubt is always there. The police haven't been any help; they just cover the bases and come up with no answers."

"And your Grandpa Roman?" Alex asked, probing the sensitive topic. Her gaze held his, a mix of caution and a desire to share, opening the door to a story not yet fully revealed.

The mention of her lost family member felt like a natural progression, a deeper dive into the heart of Brimpool's mystery, guided by Lucy's own experiences. "Grandpa was one of the good ones," she said, her hands lost in her hair, a gesture of self-comfort. "Full of life and laughter. And then. . . nothing. Just gone." Her voice wavered, the first crack in her composure Alex had seen.

At that moment, Alex reminded himself that Grandpa Roman was not just a name to add to his article; he was a loved one missed, a reminder of the human cost behind the vanishings. This revelation, shared in the quiet aftermath of their night together, underscored the complexity of the story he had come to excavate, intertwining the pursuit of truth with the acknowledgment of personal loss and resilience.

"They said he probably just left, started a new life somewhere," Lucy explained, a hint of bitterness lacing her words. "They claim people do it all the time. But Grandpa wouldn't have just walked away. Not without saying anything to me. Not without. . ." Her voice trailed off, lost in the weight of unspoken fears and unresolved grief.

Alex sensed the depth of her frustration, how let down she felt at the dead end the police had come up with. It was a story he'd heard all too often, the official narrative falling short of revealing the nuanced realities of those left behind. "Do you have access to your grandpa's place?" he asked gently, mindful of the line he was walking between personal empathy and professional curiosity.

Lucy looked at him, assessing his intent, then nodded slowly. "Yes, we were close. I used to shop for him sometimes. I still have my key. But the police have been through the house. Why? You think you'll find something they didn't?"

"I've done some crime reporting in the past," Alex admitted. "Sometimes a fresh set of eyes can catch something. Plus, I. . .genuinely want to help, if I can." It was the truth or as much of it as he could admit to himself. The journalist in him saw a story to chase, but the human saw a chance to offer some semblance of comfort, however small.

Lucy paused, her agreement hanging in the balance, then finally gave a slight nod. "All right, we can go there. But I have to warn you," she hesitated, "there is a heaviness to that house that I can't explain."

⇒⇒⇒⫷⫷⫷

As they approached the quaint, ivy-clad facade of Grandpa Roman's house, a sense of unease wrapped around Alex. The air felt dense, humming with an energy that pricked his skin as if the very atmosphere held its breath. The home, a silent witness to the day Roman vanished, watched with windows like eyes full of secrets. The garden, with tools left as if just set down, stood neglected, and a swing hung mute, somehow moving minutely in the still air.

Entering the house was like stepping into a paused story. The living room, with its cozy, lived-in air, seemed to wait for Roman's return. His reading glasses lay forgotten on an open book, a crossword puzzle waiting to be finished. Alex, with a detective's eye, sifted through the remnants of Roman's life: family photos, a collection of sea compasses; he caught the echo of tobacco. The house whispered of Roman's presence yet hinted at mysteries lurking beneath the mundane veneer.

Lucy's voice, laden with nostalgia and loss, filled the space as she touched a set of vintage maps. "He loved these," she said, her words a bridge to Roman's world, one of unrealized dreams of travel. "I used to joke that he was more at home with the maps than the real world."

Alex, absorbing the weight of Lucy's words, offered a quiet acknowledgment. "He sounds like quite the character," he said. This shared moment, tender and filled with the gravity of loss, wove a deeper connection between them, melding their quest for answers with the poignant human story at the core of Brimpool's enigma.

"Did anything unusual happen the day he disappeared? Anything at all?" Alex probed softly, inviting Lucy to unearth any overlooked detail.

A spark of memory lit her eyes as she turned towards the kitchen. "There was something," she began, her voice threaded with a new layer of curiosity. "We found his watch on the kitchen floor. Completely unlike him; he was never without it." She retrieved the watch from a nearby drawer and handed it to Alex.

He noticed that the hands of the watch were stopped. "Do you remember the date Roman disappeared?"

She thought for a moment, and then said, "Yes. . . May 14th. It was a Saturday."

Alex held up the watch for her to see. "Did you notice this?" Looks like it stopped on the exact day he vanished."

The revelation struck a chord. The watch had possibly slipped from Roman's wrist at the critical moment he'd disappeared. This once-ordinary object might be a silent witness to the extraordinary, offering them a tangible link to the mystery shrouding Brimpool.

"Can you show me where you found the watch exactly?" Alex said.

Lucy gestured towards a forgotten corner of the kitchen, a

space now seeming more like a threshold to the unknown than a part of the home. An unnatural chill crept into the room, as though an invisible hand of ice had wrapped itself around them. It was then, amidst the growing cold, that the watch began an erratic ticking, reviving as if touched by unseen hands.

They both looked at each other, incredulous.

From behind them, a terrifying moan.

A shadow darted across the wall—swift and amorphous, as if the darkness itself had come alive.

Slicing through the suffocating silence came a whisper as sharp as a knife's edge.

"Run!"

The urgency in the spectral voice left no room for doubt. Lucy blanched, her hand clapping over her mouth in shocked recognition. The fear in her eyes confirmed it—they'd just heard Roman's voice.

No second warning was needed. Lucy fled, propelled by the visceral realization that they were not alone; the house, or what lingered within, had communicated a stark warning. Alex immediately gave chase. As they burst into the daylight, the door slammed shut behind them with grim finality, as if the house itself was sealing away its secrets once more.

In the somber quiet of Lucy's apartment, shadowed by the day's unsettling events at Roman's, Alex was cast into a different kind of darkness, his thoughts a tangled web. Their attempts to piece together what happened—whether Roman's spirit's plea or a darker force at play—only spiraled into deeper mysteries. Lucy, overwhelmed, had sought refuge in sleep, leaving Alex alone with his thoughts and the soft glow of his laptop.

Fingers poised over the keyboard, he wrestled to find words that would adequately describe their harrowing experience. How could he convey the surreal blend of fear, curiosity, and disbelief that had gripped them? It was more than just a story for Eclipse Online; it was a puzzle that deepened with every attempt to solve it.

Seeking a break, or perhaps a clue, Alex continued his search for vanished people in Brimpool, leading him down a rabbit hole of forums, news articles, and obscure blogs. It was on one such site that he stumbled upon a mention of a local support group for those affected by the vanishings. They met twice a week, with the next gathering scheduled in two days.

The discovery was a beacon in the fog of uncertainty. Here was a chance to hear other stories, to learn if what they experienced was an isolated incident or part of a larger, more complex pattern. With a renewed sense of purpose, Alex bookmarked the page, the first draft of his article momentarily forgotten. This group might hold a key to understanding the vanishings, and he was determined to unlock it.

As the night deepened, a sudden chill and encroaching shadows around him hinted at unseen eyes watching, a reminder that the mystery they chased was perhaps, in turn, chasing them.

Two days passed, each moment threading Alex and Lucy closer together. What had started as a fleeting connection in the dim light of the Salty Dragon Lounge had deepened into something more profound, an unspoken bond forged in the shadows of Grandpa Roman's haunting farewell. The chilling experience at the old house had left them with more questions than answers, yet in the search for truth, they found solace in each other's company.

Now, they ventured towards the home of Morgan Bennett, founder of a unique support group designed for individuals whose loved ones had mysteriously vanished. Alex couldn't help but feel a twinge of trepidation. What if they were about to step into a den of oddballs and conspiracy theorists?

The warm glow from Morgan's windows barely pierced the cloak of Alex's unease. Yet, as they entered, any visions of a conspiracy theorist's haven dissolved. They found themselves in a realm of warmth and understanding, a refuge for those haunted by the inexplicable. It quickly became clear that Morgan, their host, was a beacon of stability, his scholarly yet empathetic presence offering much-needed solace to this particular group. His home, brimming with texts and tomes on the esoteric and the unknown, mirrored his commitment to their cause. His welcoming demeanor, both casual and commanding, eased Alex and Lucy into the fold.

As they mingled with the group, they absorbed stories of profound loss. A mother's tale of a daughter vanished from the

THE SHUDDERING BREATH BEFORE OBLIVION

yard, a husband recounting his partner's inexplicable disappearance while making love, a brother lamenting a sibling lost on a mundane hike—all revealed in the hallowed space of Morgan's sanctuary, their collective yearning for answers a bond stronger than the mysteries that divided them.

Later, as the group nestled into the welcoming embrace of Morgan Bennett's living room, their host, assuming his place with calm authority, captured their focus with a mere clearing of his throat.

"As always, thank you all for coming tonight," Morgan began, his voice steady and imbued with a reassuring warmth that seemed to blanket the room, "For our newcomers tonight, it's important to know that our group believes that these experiences, as harrowing as they can be, aren't random occurrences. They're part of a larger pattern, a cry from the Earth itself, signaling a profound shift. We're at a tipping point, where the energy of our collective consciousness is clashing with the Earth's. These vanishings are a sign, a call to awaken to the realities we've tried so hard to ignore."

He shifted on his feet, his eyes moving between Alex and Lucy. "This is the Earth's pain made manifest, felt more intensely in areas that have suffered at the hands of pollution, neglect, or historic environmental damage. And our missing loved ones," he explained, "are part of the Earth's response to decades, if not centuries, of neglect and exploitation. It's not random; it's a selective process."

Alex and Lucy exchanged a quick, clandestine glance, their eyes mirroring a shared skepticism.

Morgan continued, "Those who vanish resonate on a frequency that aligns with this global shift—a readiness to be part of a new consciousness. It's less about loss and more about transformation. We're at a crucial juncture where the collective energy of our consciousness is at odds with the Earth's. These vanishings are a wake-up call, urging us to confront realities we've long ignored. Individuals who've 'disappeared' are now part of a different existence, one that's in harmony with the planet's vibrational shift."

Alex listened intently, his skepticism etching deeper lines across his forehead as Morgan's theory unfolded. Hesitantly, he raised a hand, pausing the discourse. "Excuse the question," he started, the room's attention pivoting towards him, "If those who've vanished were truly resonating with this. . . new consciousness, how do we reconcile experiences that suggest otherwise?" The room stilled, every gaze fixed on him as he elaborated on their unnerving encounter at Grandpa Roman's home—the spectral shadows, the stopped watch that began ticking again, the room's sudden drop in temperature, and the imperative whisper to 'run' slicing through the darkness.

Alex's tale hung suspended in the air like an ominous fog.

"What if," Alex posited, "some of those who've disappeared were actual warnings to us? Signals not of readiness but. . . of resistance? The voice we heard seemed scared, desperate to protect us from. . . whatever it was that took him."

"It's a compelling point, Alex," Morgan finally said, his voice tinged with a newfound gravity, "And yes, your experience challenges some of our assumptions. Perhaps a reminder that the phenomenon we're dealing with is complex. . . multifaceted."

He paced slowly, hands clasped behind his back, allowing the room to absorb his words. "The idea of transformation, of a shift towards a new consciousness, is an interpretation. But I'd be lying if I said we had all the answers. All the disappearances might not fit neatly into this paradigm. If some are indeed warnings or acts of resistance against this shift, it implies a diversity in how these energies interact with us."

Morgan stopped pacing, his gaze fixed on Alex and Lucy. "This isn't the first time we've discussed this perspective, but perhaps it warrants deeper exploration. Perhaps these 'signals of resistance', as you put it, are evidence of a more dynamic engagement between our world and the forces at play. Maybe they're indicative of a struggle, not just within the Earth's consciousness. . . but within humanity."

The room was silent, every member pondering Morgan's words.

"Let's consider," Morgan continued, "that both phenomena exist simultaneously. On one hand, some are, for lack of a better term, 'chosen' for transformation due to their resonance with this new vibrational shift. On the other hand, there could be individuals or energies resisting this change—such as Lucy's grandfather—manifesting as warnings or attempts to protect."

He looked around, ensuring he had everyone's attention. "This doesn't diminish the significance of either experience but rather expands our understanding. It suggests a battle of sorts, not just for the future of our planet, but for the very essence of our being."

As Morgan spoke, Alex and Lucy exchanged another glance. Their eyes, filled with doubts, silently questioned the far-reaching theories, pointing to their struggle to reconcile Morgan's words with their own unsettling experience.

"It's a lot to take in, I know," Morgan admitted softly, his tone conciliatory rather than defensive. "This journey we're on—it's filled with more questions than answers. And skepticism. . .it's not only natural but also necessary. It keeps us searching and questioning. You're here because you're seeking, and that's the first step towards understand—" Morgan's voice faltered, his frame shuddering with an intensity that echoed the shadows now stretching across the room. His eyes went wide with a terror that no words could capture, locked onto something unseen, something unfathomable.

As Morgan's form convulsed, a silent scream etched into his visage. The room plunged into a cold so biting, it seemed to slice through bone, a harbinger of unseen, malevolent forces gathering strength.

Suddenly, Morgan was no more. In his place, a void, a chilling absence where once a man had stood, shaking and afraid. The group erupted into chaos, a maelstrom of fear and disbelief as two more people were quickly plucked from their midst, swallowed by a hungry darkness that now enveloped everything.

Screams tore through the chaos as the support group fractured, its members ensnared in a nightmare. Lucy's grip on Alex was ironclad, the specter of Roman's earlier warning propelling them forward.

"Run!"

They burst into the night, the chill of the air a sharp reminder of the line between the known and the unknowable they had just crossed. Behind them, the darkness of the house loomed, a maw ready to devour all who dared to unearth its secrets.

In the aftermath of the bedlam that had torn through Morgan Bennett's home, Alex again found himself sprawled out in Lucy's apartment. It had become their makeshift command center for their fight against the creeping shadows of the night, a bulwark in the small hours when fear and doubt loomed largest. The disappearance of Brimpool's own—Morgan included, ripped from reality right before their disbelieving eyes—cast a long, ominous shroud over their haven. It was an abrupt reminder: staying in Brimpool courted danger, perhaps even death. The darkness wasn't just closing in; it was hungry.

Lucy, with the methodical determination of someone who knew they were fighting against more than just time, packed necessities into suitcases. Meanwhile, Alex, unable to shake the feeling that every second wasted was a second lost, dove back into the Internet's warren of forums, news clips, and shady blogs. His search wasn't aimless; it was a desperate search for patterns that mirrored Brimpool's nightmare.

Amidst the cacophony of online whisperings, he stumbled upon a heated debate that kept him glued to his chair—the notion that reality's fabric was wearing thin, suggesting those who disappeared worldwide were trapped in a sort of netherworld. Not just a limbo, but a place where shadows breathed and whispers carried the weight of screams. The stories from those left behind once dismissed as attempts to ward off grief suddenly formed a terrifying mosaic of evidence. Voices in the void, fleeting shadows, the sudden rush of a familiar scent—all markers of another place or dimension. Close, yet impossibly distant.

The idea wasn't just unsettling; it gnawed at the edges of Alex's sanity. Yet, it was Lucy's steady presence, her focus amidst the storm, that kept him anchored. Their heated discussions, a blend of theory and raw emotion, endured through the night. The possibility of a limbo, once an unthinkable concept, had now stitched itself into their reality. Yet theories, no matter how convincing, were cold comfort against the growing tide of disappearances that now seemed to span the globe.

As Alex pieced together the disparate threads, a pattern emerged. The vanishings were clustered around scars left by humanity on the Earth, wounds that told a story of neglect and exploitation. It painted a grim tableau: the planet, in its dying throes, perhaps claiming its due. Yet, in the heart of despair, Alex found a spark of something fierce, something that refused to bow to the dark. Hope. If he could bring this pattern to light, expose it through his words, if he could show the world the cost of its carelessness, maybe—just maybe—they could stem the tide of disappearances. It was a long shot, a Hail Mary in the face of oblivion.

The silence that hung in the room was heavy with implication. More research soon bore fruit, tying Brimpool's ecological deterioration directly to the unsettling pattern of vanishings.

"Lucy," Alex's voice cut through the stillness, a hint of excitement tinged with dread coloring his tone. "Do you remember what Morgan mentioned? About the 'Earth's pain made manifest'?"

Lucy paused her packing, a suitcase half-closed at her feet, and looked up. "Something about pollution and the environment, wasn't it?" she replied, her voice laced with a newfound seriousness.

Alex referred to his writing pad, reading from the notes he'd taken at the support group meeting. "He said the vanishings were a result of the Earth's pain made manifest. That it was felt more intensely in areas that have suffered at the hands of pollution, neglect, or historic environmental damage."

A spark of understanding flickered in Lucy's eyes as she processed his words, the pieces starting to align in her mind. "I remember now. You've found something?"

Turning to face her, Alex said, "I think it's connected to the Biosynthetix fiasco. Sound familiar?"

Realization dawned on Lucy's face. "Yes. I don't pay much attention to the news. But I remember one of my regulars at the bar convinced me to sign a petition a couple of years ago."

Alex referred to the many open tabs on his laptop. "Biosynthetix's legacy of environmental negligence is staggering. The local waterways, the wildlife—it's all been impacted. And it's not just Brimpool. This is a pattern replicated around the globe wherever there's been a flagrant disregard for nature."

A shadow of guilt passed over Lucy's features. "I'm ashamed I haven't paid more attention to this."

With a sympathetic nod, Alex looked back at his screen, a plan forming. "Eclipse has a thing for unmasking corruption. Linking this environmental crisis directly to the vanishings could be huge. With my editor Max's support, we could shine a light on Biosynthetix's actions and their consequences. If we can expose this pattern. . .not just in Brimpool, but in pockets around the world, maybe it would make a difference."

The weight of this knowledge pressing heavily on Alex's shoulders, he picked up his phone, navigating through his contacts until he found Max's number. The call went to voicemail, as he half-expected, given the late hour. "Max, it's Alex. I've come across something significant, something that could change everything we know about the vanishings in Brimpool. This goes beyond a small coastal town situation. We need to talk as soon as possible. Please, call me back the moment you get this."

He ended the call, hoping Max would sense the urgency, and responded quickly. The silence that followed was suffocating, filled with the enormity of their situation and the uncertainty of what was to come.

"And what about the police?" Lucy said.

Alex sighed, acknowledging the likelihood that someone from the support group, perhaps one survivor, might have already contacted the authorities. But uncertainty gnawed at him. "Even if someone else has already reported it, we can't just assume the police will connect the dots. They need to hear it from us too, anonymously if we have to. Just to be sure."

Lucy nodded, her eyes meeting his.

Alex stood up and closed his laptop with finality. "But first, we need a place to lie low and sort through this—away from Brimpool's reach."

Lucy nodded, understanding dawning in her eyes. "My family has an old cabin a few hours from here. It's secluded, off the grid. We could head there, maybe figure out our next move in safety."

The suggestion brought a tangible sense of relief to Alex, the weight of their shared burden momentarily lifted by the prospect of a safe haven.

"Let's get the hell out of here."

The night unfurled its dark wings, punctuated by the fleeting glow of headlights and the enigmatic shapes of the landscape rushing by. Lucy navigated the highway with a sense of urgency that mingled with the brisk air rushing through the half-opened windows. Alex sat beside her, his thoughts racing as fast as the car, cherishing each mile that widened the distance between them and the town of Brimpool.

Amidst the engine's roar and the whistling of the night wind,

THE SHUDDERING BREATH BEFORE OBLIVION

Alex wrestled with the eerie reality that had ensnared them. "All I can think about is how this situation. . .is just a reflection of all of us."

Lucy's eyes flickered towards him, her face half caught in the dim dashboard lights. Alex continued, "We take and take. . .and then act surprised when there are consequences."

They fell into silence again, each lost in their own reflections. Alex's thoughts drifted to his mother, father, and family, to the loved ones who might also vanish. "But there are good people in this world, too. People who care. People *I* care about," he murmured, the weight of concern heavy in his voice.

Lucy reached out and found Alex's hand, a simple gesture that united them against the uncertainty ahead.

Alex pondered the nascent bond forming between them in all the chaos. It was an odd sort of romance, blossoming on the precipice of an apocalypse. Ironic. Yet, in these fleeting moments of connection, he found a sliver of hope—a reason to keep fighting, to keep searching for answers.

Lost in thought, he barely noticed the change in Lucy's posture until she gasped, her breath hitching in a mix of awe and horror. Her eyes, wide and unblinking, stared through the windshield at a sight unseen to Alex.

He sat up, startled. "What is it?"

Lucy's response was barely above a whisper. "Can't you see them?" she murmured; her gaze fixed on a point somewhere in the darkness ahead.

Alex strained his eyes, searching the night for what had captured her attention. But all he saw was the empty road, the trees lining its sides like silent sentinels of the dark.

"They're there. . .trapped," Lucy continued her voice a mix of wonder and despair. "Between here and. . .somewhere else. Like Grandpa Roman," she said, a tear trailing down her cheek, "Stuck in the in-between."

And then she emitted a shuddering breath before vanishing into oblivion.

Alex's world didn't just tilt—it capsized. No skipped heartbeat—this was free-fall panic. Muscle and instinct locked in, hands snapping at the steering wheel with a grip forged in sheer terror.

The car turned rogue, a metal beast lashing out across the road.

Tires screamed a banshee's wail as Alex fought for control. The landscape blurred, a whirlwind of motion.

Adrenaline honed his focus, sharp as a blade. He muscled the wheel, feet jabbing at the pedals in a desperate dance. The car skidded in a wild tango with the asphalt, leaving a trail of burnt rubber on its compacted surface.

Then chaos weighed in. The car jerked to a stop, the engine ticking as it cooled off. Alex sat, breathing hard, trying to stitch reality back together. Silence settled, heavy, haunted by Lucy's last words, and the pounding of his heart began to slow.

"Why!?!" he screamed into the void, his voice a raw expression of grief and frustration. "What do you want from us?"

Rather than bowing to fear, a spark of resolve lit up within him. He wasn't finished—not even close. Inhaling deeply, he squared off against the enveloping gloom. It was time to move, to break the stranglehold of this terrifying reality.

Alex was set, ready to wage his war, to slice through the night's veil. His phone rang, breaking the oppressive silence. The screen displayed Max's name, a glimmer of hope in the overwhelming darkness. For a moment, Alex allowed himself to believe that maybe, just maybe, there was a way out of this nightmare. If he could just tell Max everything, and expose the truth to the world, perhaps there was still time for a solution, a way to heal the rift between humanity and nature.

But as the phone's persistent ring filled the now-empty car, it echoed in a world that no longer had anyone to answer.

THE END?

**Not if you want to dive into more of Crystal Lake Publishing's
Tales from the Darkest Depths!**

Check out our amazing website and online store
or download our latest catalog here.
https://geni.us/CLPCatalog

We always have great new projects and content on the website to dive into, as well as a newsletter, behind the scenes options, social media platforms, our own dark fiction shared-world series and our very own webstore. Our webstore even has categories specifically for KU books, non-fiction, anthologies, and of course more novels and novellas.

ABOUT THE AUTHOR

Born in 1970, in Phoenix, Arizona, Taylor Grant was a two-time Bram Stoker Award nominated author, professional screenwriter, actor, and award-winning filmmaker. His work has been seen on network television, the big screen, the stage and the web, in newspapers, comic books, national magazines and anthologies, and heard on the radio.

He started his career in children's entertainment, serving as a staff writer and development consultant for multiple production companies working on various projects, including *Beetlejuice*, *Mighty Morphin Power Rangers*, *Bad Dog*, and *Monster Farm*, which he created and co-developed for television. As development executive at Stan Lee Media, Taylor worked closely with the iconic creator, co-developing multiple web animated series, including *The Backstreet Project*, *The Accuser*, *The Drifter*, and *The 7th Portal*.

In recent years, as Head of Global Animation at Wattpad WEBTOON Studios, Taylor executive produced the animated TV series *Lore Olympus* with The Jim Henson Company and served as a Business Development Lead on the global hit anime series *Tower of God*, as well as *The God of High School*. He also produced the horror feature film *Gremoryland*, alongside Roy Lee and Vertigo Entertainment, and wrote and produced the #1 horror series *Rot & Ruin*, a WEBTOON comic adaptation of the New York Times Bestselling novel by Jonathan Maberry. He wrote and produced two short films *The Vanished* and *Sticks and Stones*, which screened at the prestigious Cannes Film Festival and received distribution through Sony and Shorts TV.

As an author Taylor shared pages with Stephen King, Neil Gaiman, Clive Barker, and many of the top writers in speculative fiction, with short fiction published in *Cemetery Dance Magazine*, *Weird Tales*, *The Siren's Call* and *Weirdbook* and in numerous anthologies. His first collection of short stories, *The Dark at the End of the Tunnel* (2015, Crystal Lake Publishing), became an instant Amazon bestseller and was nominated for two Bram Stoker Awards, for 'Best Collection' and for 'Best Short Story' ('The Infected'). His second collection, *The Many Deaths of Cole Parker* was published in 2020 by Running Wild Press. *The Shuddering Breath Before Oblivion*, a final tribute to Taylor, collects the last of his short fiction. Taylor died on September 12th, 2024.

Readers . . .

Thank you for reading *The Shuddering Breath Before Oblivion.*
We hope you enjoyed this collection.

If you have a moment, please review *The Shuddering Breath
Before Oblivion* at the store where you bought it.

Help other readers by telling them why you enjoyed this book.
No need to write an in-depth discussion. Even a single sentence
will be greatly appreciated. Reviews go a long way to helping a
book sell, and is great for an author's career. It'll also help us to
continue publishing quality books.

Thank you again for taking the time to journey with Crystal Lake
Publishing.

Visit our Linktree page for a list of our social media platforms.
https://linktr.ee/CrystalLakePublishing

Follow us on Amazon:

MISSION STATEMENT:

Since its founding in August 2012, Crystal Lake has quickly become one of the world's leading publishers of Dark Fiction and Horror books. In 2023, Crystal Lake officially transitioned into an entertainment company, joining several other divisions, genres, and imprints, including Torrid Waters, Crystal Lake Comics, Crystal Lake Games, Crystal Lake Kids, and many more.

While we strive to present only the highest quality fiction and entertainment, we also endeavour to support authors along their writing journey. We offer our time and experience in non-fiction projects, as well as author mentoring and services, at competitive prices.

With several Bram Stoker Award wins and many other wins and nominations (including the HWA's Specialty Press Award), Crystal Lake Publishing puts integrity, honor, and respect at the forefront of our publishing operations.

We strive for each book and outreach program we spearhead to not only entertain and touch or comment on issues that affect our readers, but also to strengthen and support the Dark Fiction field and its authors.

Not only do we find and publish authors we believe are destined for greatness, but we strive to work with men and women who endeavour to be decent human beings who care more for others than themselves, while still being hard working, driven, and passionate artists and storytellers.

Crystal Lake Publishing is and will always be a beacon of what passion and dedication, combined with overwhelming teamwork and respect, can accomplish. We endeavour to know each and every one of our readers, while building personal relationships with our authors, reviewers, bloggers, podcasters, bookstores, and libraries.

We will be as trustworthy, forthright, and transparent as any business can be, while also keeping most of the headaches away from our authors, since it's our job to solve the problems so they can stay in a creative mind. Which of course also means paying our authors.

We do not just publish books, we present to you worlds within your world, doors within your mind, from talented authors who sacrifice so much for a moment of your time.

There are some amazing small presses out there, and through collaboration and open forums we will continue to support other presses in the goal of helping authors and showing the world what quality small presses are capable of accomplishing. No one wins when a small press goes down, so we will always be there to support hardworking, legitimate presses and their authors. We don't see Crystal Lake as the best press out there, but we will always strive to be the best, strive to be the most interactive and grateful, and even blessed press around. No matter what happens over time, we will also take our mission very seriously while appreciating where we are and enjoying the journey.

What do we offer our authors that they can't do for themselves through self-publishing?

We are big supporters of self-publishing (especially hybrid publishing), if done with care, patience, and planning. However, not every author has the time or inclination to do market research, advertise, and set up book launch strategies. Although a lot of authors are successful in doing it all, strong small presses will always be there for the authors who just want to do what they do best: write.

What we offer is experience, industry knowledge, contacts and trust built up over years. And due to our strong brand and trusting fanbase, every Crystal Lake Publishing book comes with weight of respect. In time our fans begin to trust our judgment and will try a new author purely based on our support of said author.

With each launch we strive to fine-tune our approach, learn from our mistakes, and increase our reach. We continue to assure our authors that we're here for them and that we'll carry the weight of the launch and dealing with third parties while they focus on their strengths—be it writing, interviews, blogs, signings, etc.

We also offer several mentoring packages to authors that include knowledge and skills they can use in both traditional and self-publishing endeavours.

We look forward to launching many new careers.

This is what we believe in. What we stand for. This will be our legacy.

Welcome to Crystal Lake Publishing— Where stories come alive!